THE GLASS HOUSE

BETTINA WOLFE

The Glass House

Cover design by Stuart Bache

To my mom, with love.

The cruelest lies are often told in silence.
—Robert Louis Stevenson

PROLOGUE

I gaze at your body lying twisted on the ground. It wasn't supposed to end this way. I promised you a life of love, not pain—a life of happiness, not sorrow.

Your suffering is over and has now shifted to me.

I don't know what I'll do without you. I don't know if I will ever forgive myself—this house or this place.

We were meant to be together forever.

Valerie

I had never believed in love at first sight until the day that mysterious stranger walked into my life.

We met when I worked as a cocktail server in Vegas, the absolute worst job on the planet for someone like me, but I needed money, and the money was good. I don't know how I tolerated the nonsense that went along with it... the drunkards, the serial cheaters, and the married old geezers who thought they could buy you with a wad of hundreds or a stack of chips. At times it was too much to handle.

Then one night, David appeared. Not only was he handsome, but there was also something different about him. He was unlike the others who visited the lounge. He wasn't your typical obnoxious drunk, slurring his words while snapping his fingers in the air, demanding service. I guessed him to be in his late forties, give or take, judging from the flecks of gray in his thick head of hair. And I didn't notice a gold band or the telltale white line around his ring finger.

I remember him sitting there through the haze of cigarette and cigar smoke, dressed casually in dark jeans and a black polo shirt. He kept to himself while sipping an almost empty glass of Merlot. The moment I approached him, he smiled genuinely, deep lines wrinkling around dark brown, almond-shaped eyes.

"Care for another?" I asked, returning a slight smile of my own.

"Sure, thanks," he replied, swirling the last of the wine in his glass.

As I walked away, I could feel his eyes on me watching my every move. Typically when men stared, it would creep me out, especially the way they would leer at me up and down. Of course, the ridiculous uniforms we had to wear didn't help either, too short, too tight, and way too revealing for my taste. It was the most uncomfortable piece of polyester I ever wore that didn't breathe in the desert heat. I was a hot, sweaty mess in that costumed get-up. But it was only for a year—at least that's what I had told myself.

I first started working at the Sky Royal Hotel as a front desk representative. That uniform, a navy blue pantsuit—another polyester garment, better matched my personality—

buttoned-up and conservative. But Cindy, my roommate, had been a cocktail server for two years and made triple my salary. While she collected tips, hundreds a day for slinging cocktails, I checked guests in and out of their rooms for a few hundred a week.

"Just apply for the darn job before someone else fills the last opening," Cindy had said, shaking a bottle of crimson nail polish. "Do you know how many girls are vying for the position? Besides, I'm tired of hearing you complain about never having enough money," she quipped. She quickly finished painting her long pointy nails as she prepared for her shift.

"Okay, okay," I groaned, "I'll apply."

Pursing her lips, she blew short breaths of air onto each of her fingernails. After waving her hands in the air, she strategically grabbed her keys and handbag, rushing out the door.

Two weeks later, thanks to Cindy, I was the newest yet one of the oldest cocktail servers in the Crystal Lounge. While I was thirty-two, I was thankful I could pass for twenty-five. Cindy had warned me about the 'secret rules' of the server girls. First rule—no one over thirty ever qualified for the job. Second rule—no fraternizing with the hotel guests. If you did, you had better keep it to yourself, and if it went any further, never kiss and tell. It was grounds for immediate termination.

Thank goodness those days are behind me. I've traded

toe-pinching high heels and itchy uniforms for a wardrobe of flip-flops, T-shirts, and shorts.

When I had brought David his second glass of Merlot that night, he reached into his pocket and retrieved a business card.

"I hope this doesn't sound too forward, but I'd like to take you out for dinner sometime," he said, gazing up at me.

I stood there, balancing the tray in my hand, contemplating a reply as he stared at my chest.

"I'm here for the week, so you only have five days to choose from." Squinting his eyes, he flashed me a half smile. "Sorry, I don't have my reading glasses with me. Is it Valerie?"

I realized he was trying to read my name tag pinned slightly above my left breast.

"Yes, it is," I replied, inching my free hand to my chest. "But my friends call me Val."

As I leaned over, setting the glass on the table, he reached up and placed his card on my tray.

"Nice to meet you, Val." Another smile. "Listen, I'll understand if you say no or have to think about it," he winked.

I gave the card a cursory glance. *David Radferd, International Sales Director, Limón Export.*

"I'll think about it," I said, turning away.

The following night, I had just begun my shift at the Crystal Lounge. As I stood at the bar picking up an order, I carefully organized the drinks on my tray by glass size and volume. When I turned around to head over to a table of guests, I almost bumped right into him.

"Oh, David, hi!" I took a step back, gripping the tray as liquids swayed, the drinks spilling over their rims. In an instant, he reached out, steadying my hands to help save the glasses from falling.

"Sorry about that, I didn't mean to startle you."

"It's okay," I said, now holding the tray with both hands. I took another step to the side. "Are you stalking me?"

"No, no," he declared, shaking his head. Pointing over his shoulder with his thumb, I noticed three men sitting at a table.

"I'm with a few business associates. We stopped by for a drink before dinner."

"Okay, well, that's not my section, but I'm sure someone will be right with you."

"Speaking of dinner, I wanted to remind you that you only have four days left to choose from," he leaned in slightly, eyes smiling.

I gazed at him for a few seconds, up and down, just as men do to women. I couldn't deny an attraction to him, but I wasn't sure it was worth risking my job. I stood there for a moment in thought. *Oh, what the heck—it's only dinner—a girl's gotta eat.*

"I'm off tomorrow night. It's the only time I'm available."

"Sounds good. Where shall we meet?"

"Not here," I stated, "definitely not here. I could be fired if my supervisor found out."

"I don't want to get you in trouble," he said, raising his eyebrows.

"As long as we meet someplace else, it should be fine."

"Well, one of the guys is staying at The Amethyst. He mentioned the steakhouse is pretty good. We could meet there, say around seven. Will that work for you, Ms. Valerie? I don't even know your last name."

"Seven's fine, and my last name is Vinnello. Now, if you'll please excuse me, I have drinks to serve."

"See you tomorrow, Ms. Vinnello. I look forward to getting to know you." Flashing a smile, he turned and walked back to his table.

Our dinner conversation along with a bottle of wine flowed freely that evening. David told me about his work, his travels to Central America, and about wanting to move there to a small house and live a quiet life in the jungle. He said he had grown tired of living in one place and welcomed a change of scenery.

I shared my longing to live by the ocean again as I wasn't

much of a desert person. I had only moved to Las Vegas after running into Cindy, an old coworker from back home. She would tell me these wild, crazy stories and talk about all of the fun she was having since moving to Vegas. She practically begged me to move in with her and rent a house together. I told her I'd give it a year to see if it was the right place for me.

Two years later, however, sweating through multiple days of one hundred and fifteen degrees, I was ready to move somewhere else. I planned to save as much money as I could and move to California. Since I had lived by the Atlantic Ocean for most of my life, I thought it would be nice to see sunsets in the Pacific.

It was coincidental when David shared that he lived just outside of LA as he loved the ocean too. Despite our age difference, we seemed to have a lot in common.

"You should come to LA and visit me sometime," he said, handing me a spoon and nudging his crème brûlée toward me.

"I'd love to," I reacted a bit too quickly, the wine obviously talking for me. "It's been so long since I've stuck my toes in the sand and sat by the ocean." Scooping up a spoonful of the custard, I savored its sweetness as the caramelized sugar melted on my tongue.

"What about next weekend?" he asked. "Monday's a holiday, and I'll be home for three days… alone, unless you care to join me." Reaching for his wine, he took a long sip while staring at me over the rim of his glass.

"I do have a few vacation days saved up. I guess I could find someone to cover my shifts."

Did I just say yes? Where are these words coming from? Note to self: Do not drink half a bottle of wine among strangers.

"Great, I can't wait." He beamed, his eyes lighting up as if he had hit the jackpot.

The waiter came over and politely asked if we needed anything else.

"I'd like a cup of black coffee, please," I requested. I needed it to stave off the effects of too much wine and sugar.

"Make that two," David added, "with a side of cream."

When the waiter turned away, David rested his arms on the table, palms up.

"Give me your hands," he instructed, wiggling his fingers.

I glanced to my left and then to my right, checking to see if anyone was watching us.

"Why?"

"Just do as I say," he pleaded, his gaze lingering.

Unwillingly, I stretched out my arms, placing my hands next to his. He slowly curled his fingers around mine, massaging the sides of my palms with his thumbs.

"Now, this may sound a bit strange, but I feel as if we've met before."

"But… we… haven't," I said, drawing out each word and lowering my head.

"It's as if I've known you in another lifetime... as if we were destined to meet again."

At that point, it had sounded like the wine was talking for him too.

"Really?" I half giggled. "I bet you say that to all the women you meet."

"I'm serious. I feel a strong pull when I'm near you."

Holding his gaze, I felt a spark pulsate through my arms. I couldn't deny it. I did feel *something* as he held onto my hands, a warm, peaceful feeling that connected us, binding us together. It was as if, at that moment, I happened to be in the right place at the right time.

The waiter soon returned with our coffee, setting the cups down near the edge of the table, careful not to disturb our interlocked arms.

David nodded at him and turned back to me, keeping a firm grip on my hands.

2

David

This one is different; she has potential—a diamond in the rough. I like that Valerie isn't reed-thin. Her chocolate brown hair and voluptuous curves are a breath of fresh air. She's so unlike the painstakingly thin Barbie dolls that travel in flocks in this city. Sure they're cute, but they could all use a good meal.

Not my Val, though, she's no 'Valley girl.' Not only did she eat a meal I paid for, but she also indulged in a dessert with me—a rarity. I can't remember the last time I shared something sweet with someone. Val is a great gal. She's someone who can keep up with me.

I glance at my watch and realize she'll be here any

minute. I check the room one last time, making sure everything's put away. I wouldn't want her discovering items from my past… from my previous life. It's too much information too soon.

I feel a vibration in my pocket as my cell phone buzzes against my thigh. Sliding it out, I gaze down and see a text message.

I'm here, out front. Hope I'm at the right place. Val

Oh, you're at the right place, all right. You're home. I'm tempted to text back. But instead, I slink down the stairs with my head held high, thoughts swirling, excited as I open the front door.

"There she is," I reach for her overnight bag. "How was the drive?" I ask, and then smile.

"Not bad, it took me a little over five hours. I followed the GPS and made a few pit stops along the way."

"You've never been to California?" I tilt my head ever so suavely.

"No, it's my first time."

"Really? For some reason, I thought you had been here before."

She follows me inside, up the stairs, and into the living room. I place her luggage down and then turn to her, enveloping her in my signature bear hug. Her body feels rigid, reluctant at first, but then her hands gently press against my lower back as she returns my gesture of affection.

"I've missed you," I lean back to stare into her eyes.

"It's only been a week," she remarks, breaking away from our embrace. "Besides, you don't know me well enough to miss me." Her gaze travels across the room and along the walls, studying each and every frame for a few moments.

"Wow, these pictures are stunning." She inches her way closer to them.

"Thanks. I'm a pretty good photographer if I say so myself."

"You took all these?"

"Yes, over the years of my travels."

"So, they were all taken in Central America."

"Costa Rica to be exact."

"The waterfalls, the jungle, all these colorful birds… they're all so—exotic."

"Glad you like them."

"I do. I'm trying to imagine what it would be like to see it all in person—to experience the rushing sound of the waterfall, the birds chirping, and the earthy smell of rain in the air."

"Can I get you something to drink?" I ask. Glancing over, I study her as she stands by the waterfall photo.

"All that's missing is a tropical drink in my hand," I hear her say.

"I have a better idea. You must be hungry from all the driving, so why don't we head out for a late lunch, early dinner. We can go down to the marina and relax by the water."

"Sounds wonderful, but first, I'd like to freshen up a bit."

"Down the hall and to the right is the spare bedroom. It connects with your own private bathroom. Take as much time as you need."

"Thanks. I won't be long."

I watch as she picks up her luggage and saunters down the hallway. I must say the jeans she's wearing hug every inch of her in all the right places.

We enter one of my local haunts, The Wharf Bar and Grill, standing in the foyer waiting to be seated. To our left, local patrons perched on stools along the bar sit nursing their assorted drinks.

"Table for two?" the petite, bored-looking hostess asks.

"Yes," I reply, "outside, please, by the water."

We follow the young woman outside to the patio with a scenic view of the harbor. I take a seat next to Val. A waitress appears, placing two menus on the table and then walks away. Only two nearby tables are occupied.

At one table, a middle-aged couple sits across from each other, sharing an appetizer. At the other, two young blonde women sit close to each other in deep conversation. I glance briefly at both tables and then turn to look at Val.

"Thanks for picking this place," she says. "It's so serene; it's just what I needed."

"I thought it would do the trick, noticing how entranced you were with the waterfall photo."

She smiles at me and then peeks at the menu. The waitress soon interrupts us, apologizing, and takes our order.

"So how long have you lived in Vegas?" I ask.

"Too long," she says, rolling her eyes, "a little more than two years now."

"By the sound of your voice, I take it that it's not working out for you."

"It's not. That town is definitely not for me. I have only two friends I can trust, one of them my roommate."

"I imagine it would be tough dating in Sin City. I've been visiting Vegas the past couple of years for conventions but only stay a few days at a time. I assume living there is not all it's cracked up to be."

"That's putting it mildly; it's the land of twenty-four-seven entertainment with constant distractions. The bright lights, the so-called 'glitz and glamour,'" she air quotes the words, "not my style. I suppose, though, if you're into dating cheaters or addicts, then you'd be in the right place," she sighs.

"Ouch, it's that bad?"

"Well, I can't vouch for anyone else, but sadly that has been my experience so far."

"Think of it this way, if you didn't live in the land of glitter and garbage and hadn't waited on me that day, we would never have met."

"Yeah, I suppose you could look at it that way." Her lips curl up in a cautious smile.

Leaning into the table, I place my hand on top of hers. "You have the most beautiful eyes I've ever seen—so deep and soulful."

"Thank you," she replies, fidgeting in her seat, "must be the eyeliner."

"No, your eyes reveal your inner soul. I can see the light shining behind them."

The waitress returns with our food, placing a shrimp salad in front of Val and a bacon cheeseburger in front of me. I look up at her and order two piña coladas before she turns away.

"I believe someone mentioned something about a tropical drink earlier," I wink at Val.

"Are you trying to get me drunk and take advantage of me?"

"Only if you'll allow me to." I smile devilishly at her.

"So, enough of me," she says, changing the subject. "Tell me something about you. Any family—brothers or sisters?"

"Nope, I was orphaned at a young age."

"I'm sorry, do you want to tell me about it."

"Not really, next question."

"Have you ever been married?"

Leaning back in my chair, I release a long breath while collecting my thoughts. They all seem to ask me that one.

"I've been in a few relationships. Unfortunately, none of them worked out."

"Oh, why not?"

"It seems I've never really had a clear picture of the type of woman I'm looking for."

"So, you were married then."

Picking up the burger with one hand, I take a bite of it and flash the peace sign.

"Two times?" her brows knit together. "You've been married twice? What happened? Why didn't they work out?" she glares at me.

"As I said," taking another bite of my burger, I chew it quickly and swallow. "I haven't found the right woman yet."

She glances down, and I see her staring at my untouched French fries. I slowly slide the plate closer to her.

"What about you? Have you ever been married?"

She munches a fry and then swipes another one. "Nope, never made that mistake, thankfully."

"Mistake?" I let out a laugh. "Honestly, I'm surprised someone like you is still on the market."

She picks up her drink and takes a long sip. I catch her rolling her eyes again.

"Would you please excuse me," she says, abruptly. "I need to go powder my nose." Sliding her chair back, she stands up and reaches for her purse.

"The ladies room is behind the bar and on the left," I add, directing her.

While waiting for Val to return, I gaze out at the harbor,

admiring the boats moored in perfect lines. Some of them are yachts, which of course, I can't afford... yet.

But I'm definitely going to need a boat. It's always been part of the plan. I'm thinking of a sailboat; it's more my style anyway. I'll have to learn to sail it from here and down along the coast. I'm sure it can't be that difficult, as long as I keep the shoreline in view.

Speaking of views, the two blonde girls keep looking my way. Maybe they think I'm looking at them. I'm not, although I used to check out young women like them, wearing high heels and tight-fitting outfits, showing it all off and leaving little to the imagination.

I smile back as the one on the right twirls her long, silky hair while gazing in my direction. I've still got it. I know I look good for my age. I eat right, take supplements, and work out every day.

But those young women, while cute, are not what I want. Not this time. Those types of gals wish for someone to pay their bills and keep them accustomed to the highfalutin lifestyles they follow on social media. They'll whine if they don't get their way or what they want. I don't have time for those types this time around. I've had my fill.

I remind myself that those days are over, a thing of the past. Today I'm on a date with a woman I can talk to, a woman who listens, one I can control—a woman who could be the one.

I gaze over at the gals one last time. Now they're both staring in my direction. *Focus, you need to focus.*

When Val returns, I can see the look in her eye. Unfortunately, it isn't the look she was giving me before she left the table. No, it's 'the look,' the one that starts arguments. I know it all too well because I've seen it too many times before. Why are women so damn insecure?

But I'm not going there today. Nope, I'm not going to do it. Today of all days, I'm not in the mood to argue.

As I reach into my pocket for my wallet, I see Val chewing the tip of the plastic straw in her now empty piña colada.

"Are you ready to go?" I ask, throwing a fifty dollar bill on the table.

3

Valerie

Although I had planned to stay in California for the long weekend, I only stayed one night. When we arrived back at David's condo, I told him I wasn't feeling well—that the food didn't agree with me. I slept in the spare room and left, sneaking out early the next morning, so he wouldn't hear me leave. He was passed out and snoring so loud that the sounds of him sawing wood filled the whole house.

Once out the door, I grabbed a coffee at a little cafe two blocks from his condo and then headed for home.

I don't think he realized how long I was standing behind him in the restaurant. I saw everything—the way he stared down those two young women, the exchange of sly smiles, the blatant flirting between them. It probably shouldn't have bothered me as much as it did, but I saw it as a red flag, one of many…

The first red flag was the fact that he'd been married. Once would probably have been a warning—a yellow flag. But twice? To think he has two ex-wives somewhere out there. I wasn't interested in being someone's girl number three.

What was that line he spewed? 'I haven't found the right woman yet.' Oh, please, spare me. He had more than one chance to get it right.

The second red flag was that he was handsome—tall, dark hair, dark eyes, with a slender, athletic body. He had that sort of low-key, laid-back charm about him and was the outgoing type, maybe a little too much so. He had no problem attracting the ladies, young and old, with or without my presence. He appeared to fit the mold as most women's type.

The third red flag was that he traveled for his job—a lot. He stayed in four-star hotels when attending conventions. After work, I imagined his evening dinners with colleagues easily transitioning into drink-filled nights that conveniently included young, single women. I knew the story all too well. I had seen it play out many times at the hotel—married men and the hired 'party girls' to entertain them. Their poor, clueless wives back home. It was beyond disgraceful.

You'd think with three red flags, I would have deleted his number from my phone. He had sent me five texts while

I was driving, which I didn't reply to. But then he called me the minute I got home. When my cell phone rang, I accidentally hit the wrong button.

"I was worried about you," he said. "You left in such a hurry. I wanted to make sure you made it home safely."

Of course, it was the gentlemanly thing to do, considering I had just spent twelve out of twenty-four hours driving back and forth for a man I barely knew.

"I feel bad you drove all this way for one night. I'd like to make it up to you."

I had sensed a hint of remorse in his voice.

"Was it something I said? Something I did?" he had asked on the phone that night. I didn't feel the need to tell him or bring up the situation. It wasn't worth it, so I just let it go and kept to my story of not feeling well.

I had thought we were off to a good start. Throughout my life, I mostly dated men my age. Since he was a decade older than me, I thought it would be nice to be with someone a little older and a little wiser. Being an old soul myself, I thought I might have found my match.

"We were having such a great time," he added. "We were supposed to hang out at the beach today and watch the sunset together."

I thanked him for dinner, sharing my disappointment about missing the sunset on the beach.

"Maybe another time," I said, quickly ending the call.

Who was I kidding? The moment my words hit the air, I planned on never seeing him again.

On Tuesday afternoon, at the hotel, I was on my way to the employee break room when I ran into Nicole, one of the cocktail servers.

"Lucky lady," she said in passing, as she headed down the hallway.

"What are you talking about?"

"You'll see," she called out, disappearing around the corner.

Upon entering the room, there sat a large vase of red-tipped yellow roses. Someone had placed a sticky note on the vase with a smiley face and my name written on it. As I leaned over, inhaling the fragrance, I noticed a tiny envelope tied to the ribbon around the vase. Slipping the card out, I squinted to read the small print.

'Let's start over, xo, David.'

I wasn't sure what to think but was thankful my supervisor wasn't around to play a game of fifty questions. I hoped Nicole would keep her big mouth shut and cover for me until I could take them out of there after my shift.

When I walked through the front door of my rental after midnight, Cindy was lying on the sofa watching TV.

"Ooh, pretty! Looks like someone has an admirer," she

trilled. Sitting up to reach for the remote, she turned the volume down. "Do tell."

"They're from David with a note that read, 'let's start over.'" I set the vase on the dining table.

"Are you going to give him a second chance?" she asked, picking up her phone.

"I don't know. I'm too tired to think about it right now." Kicking off my shoes, I flopped down on the sofa beside her.

"Hey, listen to this. Yellow means happiness, friendship, and new beginnings."

"But these have red tips... so what does that mean?"

"Let's see," she said, tapping her fingernails on the screen. "According to this site, it says friendship deepening to love." She looked over at me, making googly-eyes. "Maybe he's falling in love?"

"Well, if he is, he's a little too late."

"Oh, come on, Val, give the guy a chance. He can't be any worse than the string of losers you've dated. You know you're never going to find a decent guy in this town. Not one that will live up to your standards," she added.

"Are you saying I have high standards?" I huffed.

"No, you just did."

She's right; I had set the bar high. I had pretty much given up on dating. The only time I had ever been in love was a decade ago.

My first boyfriend was my high school sweetheart, a seven year relationship that lasted six years too long. During those years, I must've worn the thickest pair of rose-colored glasses ever made.

All the girls loved Joey. He was one of a few, if not the cutest boy in school. Joey knew he was hot with his olive skin and mop of black hair. He had asked me out for junior prom, and upon graduation, we moved in together.

At the time, we had nothing but love between us, or so I thought. I worked at the mall selling cosmetics, and Joey worked construction. Every Friday we'd go out for dinner and then dancing. We both loved to dance and spent many weekends in downtown nightclubs, drinking and dancing the night away. "You're so much fun when you drink," he would say, his all-time favorite line.

Some people have innocent fun when they drink and become the life of the party... giddy, happy drunks. Not Joey. When Joey drank, his mood darkened, and he became possessive. When Joey got drunk, he became mean—nasty mean, dangerously mean. In his fits of jealous rage, I would duck and dodge as he hurled toasters and knives through the air. In his darkest times, he would threaten me, marking his territory and anger all over my body. In the middle of summer, I had no choice but to wear long-sleeved shirts to hide the deep purple bruises that covered my arms.

Our relationship ended with one final blow to my head. I had blacked out and was rushed to the hospital one cold, winter night. His balled-up fist coming straight at my face was the last I ever saw of him.

At times, when I focus on the scar in the mirror,

marking my face, I'm reminded of a relationship gone bad. Even though it had happened long ago, I haven't been able to trust men and their motives fully. After that one and a few other failed relationships, my faith in men had been tainted.

"Hey, you okay," I heard Cindy say off in the distance.

"Yeah, I'm fine," I said, massaging my forehead.

"You were in another zone, completely checked out of our conversation."

"Sorry, flashback," I got up from the sofa and drifted to the kitchen for a glass of water.

"Don't you just hate those?"

Cindy didn't know about Joey or my past, and I was too tired and ashamed to share. I always hated to think of myself as an abused victim.

"Did you at least send him a text to thank him for the flowers?"

"No, didn't have a chance as I was slammed at work."

"Well, personally, I wouldn't let a guy who looks like that slip away so fast."

How does she know what he looks like? She's never met him.

"How do you know what he looks like?" I asked perplexed.

"I googled him."

"You googled him? Why?"

"I don't know, curious, I guess."

I paused for a moment and stared at the TV.

"So what exactly does he do at Lemon Export? Export lemons?" She laughed.

"You mean Limón." Rolling my eyes, I shook my head. "It's pronounced like this, 'lee' and 'mon'... together."

"Whatever."

"Sales, from his title."

At one a.m., Cindy was wide awake and trying to keep the conversation going. But at that point, I wanted to be alone, listen to some meditation music, and drift off to sleep.

As I entered my bedroom, I unclasped my necklace and walked over to my dresser. Draping my butterfly pendant over my open jewelry box, I glanced down and saw David's business card inside.

Cindy must have been snooping around my room while I was gone. *That's so unlike her*, I had thought. Why the sudden interest in my life and the men I'm dating?

4

David

I stand in the living room, swirling a glass of Merlot, admiring the toucan on my wall. I think back to the day when I took the photo, recalling the moments leading up to the shot. I had that beautiful bird eating out of the palm of my hand. Mango, if I remember correctly.

I reflect on this past weekend. I almost had Val eating from my hand—almost had her where I wanted her. But instead of us enjoying a lazy Sunday together, she flew the coop.

Taking a long sip of wine, I savor the flavor in my mouth. The fruity sweetness zaps me back to the present moment.

A day has passed, and no word from Val. I'm sure she's received the flowers I sent. I tracked the order, so I know they were delivered. I hope I didn't cause any trouble for her at the hotel as I had no other place to send them.

Should I call or maybe text her? Or will she think I'm stalking her again? That's the strange thing about women, if you come on too strong, you're accused of harassment. If you wait a day or two, they think you've lost interest. Such beautiful but complicated beings they are.

But not my Val, she can be trained. I saw it the moment I looked into her eyes—her big, beautiful hazel eyes. They mesmerize me. Behind her eyes shines a bright, beautiful soul. I need her. I need light in my life to wash away the darkness.

I never intended to go to the dark side; the dark side found me. One taste was all it took. One enchanted evening my interest was piqued by a world unknown to me. It soon became my obsession. From the moment I awoke until the wee hours of the morning, I was consumed. I couldn't get enough. I had to know more. Deeper and deeper, I searched, absorbing the information. I never knew such things existed, hiding in plain sight. Some days it was too hard to take. It was all too consuming. There are things I wish I had never seen, never stumbled upon. But now it's too late. Pandora's box had been opened.

I need something to ease the pain. Rather, someone. I need someone real—someone I can hold onto, someone who is pure and full of light.

Val.

Beyond the light she holds inside, I feel she's hiding a deep, emotional pain from the past. I sense she's been hurt before, and afraid to trust again, but she can trust me. I'm a man to be trusted. This time it will be different. I'm ahead of the curve. I am more prepared. Yes, that's the word, prepared. I've done my research. The only thing missing is someone to share it with.

Someone I can trust with all my heart. Someone who will never share my deepest, darkest secrets.

5

Valerie

As I sat at the breakfast nook, the late morning sun streamed through the window, warming my bare shoulders. Still dressed in my pajamas, I searched the internet while drinking my third cup of coffee. Cindy had just gone to pick up a few groceries since I was out of almond milk, and she was craving waffles. I had the whole house to myself and reveled in those moments.

Cindy, the extrovert, always had to be doing something with someone and frequently invited people over when she wasn't working. I had been surprised to find her home alone that night, when David sent me flowers, and even more surprised by her interest in him.

Scrolling the site on my laptop, I found the photo Cindy must have seen. David standing among a few other men, surrounded by tall, dense trees, somewhere deep in the jungle. I zoomed in for a close-up of the photo. One of the men appeared to have a machete attached to his belt. I shuddered at the sight of it.

The website for Limón Export was colorful yet simple and had articles about coffee and tropical fruits. As I sat, sipping my coffee, I scrolled through numerous photos of banana and coffee plantations. Pausing, I glanced at the empty fruit bowl on the kitchen counter, wishing we had some bananas and hoping Cindy had written them on her shopping list.

Toward the bottom of the page was another photo of David. He was feeding a toucan perched on his arm, something orange and cubed. Mango maybe? It reminded me of the toucan photo in his condo, and I wondered if it was the same bird.

I clicked on the word 'gallery' and my screen filled with beautiful photos of lush greenery, rolling hills, volcanic mountains, and cloud forests. As I momentarily gazed over my shoulder out the window at the arid brown desert behind me, I saw a lonely cactus next to a dried out shrub in desperate need of water. I closed my eyes to imagine a different scene like the one on the screen—one with greener palm trees and sparkling blue water. I couldn't remember the last time I enjoyed a tropical vacation.

Years ago, when I lived on the East coast, my girlfriends

and I would make our annual trek to the Caribbean Islands. It was our way of surviving the long, cold New England winters. We needed something to look forward to for a week, someplace to swap our snowsuits for swimsuits.

Each year we chose a different island and took turns deciding our destination. Back then, I had fallen in love with St. Martin, my dream island getaway.

One memorable trip had tempted me to pack my bags and book a one-way ticket to the island. I figured I could find a job bartending at a thatched-roof bar and run around barefoot in the sand. Live a simple, carefree life.

I gazed back at my computer and opened a new browser tab. This time I searched for beaches in Costa Rica. As the pictures loaded, long stretches of sand and aqua blue water appeared with swaying palm trees lining the shore. Closing my eyes, it took me back to another place, another time. *What I'd give for a vacation right about now.*

My cell phone buzzing along the table interrupted my brief, online, virtual vacation. I glanced at the screen.

David.

I watched as it buzzed three more times while inching its way toward me. I decided to answer.

"Hello."

"Val? Hey, it's David."

"Hey," I replied, leaning back on the bench.

"You busy? Did I catch you at a bad time?"

"No, what's up?"

"I was calling to see how you're doing and ask if you received the flowers I sent."

"Yes, thank you." I reached for a throw pillow, stuffing it behind my back for support.

"Listen, I owe you a beach and a sunset," he blurted out after a moment of silence.

"You don't owe me anything."

"No, really, I do. I have a proposal."

I couldn't imagine what he was about to say.

"I'm heading down to Costa Rica in two weeks, and I'd like you to join me."

I stared at my computer screen, the blue waters and beaches tempting me. *He can't be serious.*

"Val, you still there?"

"It sounds nice but, umm, we just met. We hardly know each other."

"I realize that but you'll be safe with me. You'll have your own private room. No pressure. You can relax at the beach during the day while I work. In the evening, we can have dinner and watch sunsets together. All expenses paid. What do you say?"

I didn't know what to say. I glanced around the kitchen, looking for hidden cameras. It felt as though I was being set up for a reality TV show, and 'Strange Coincidences' could have been its title.

"It would be great to get away, but I'd have to find someone to cover my shifts."

"Well, think about it and let me know. I'd love the company and the chance to make it up to you."

"I appreciate the offer." I wondered if he sensed the smile growing on my face.

"Listen, I gotta run. I have a busy day ahead of me. I hope to hear from you soon."

And just like that, my tropical vacation appeared out of thin air and onto the table, awaiting an answer.

Moments later, the front door opened and closed, and the flapping of flip flops headed my way. Cindy appeared in the kitchen with four plastic grocery bags hooked on her arms.

"Remind me never to go shopping on Wednesdays," she said, setting the bags on the counter. "It was jam-packed. I waited in line forever."

Rising from the bench, I helped her unpack the food items.

"So, you're not going to believe what just happened," I said, removing a bottle of maple syrup from the bag.

"What? What did I miss?" Tearing open the flap of a box of waffles, she placed two in the toaster.

"David just called and invited me to go to Costa Rica with him."

"Get out of town!" she squealed, bouncing on her toes.

"Exactly what I'd like to do, but I don't know if I should go. I just—"

"Hell, if you don't go, I will. I can be packed and ready

in less than an hour. I only need a couple of bikinis and cut-offs."

"Ha, ha, very funny," I said. Of course it's something she would do. And wear.

"So seriously, are you going to go?"

"I kinda want to."

"Well, you already survived a night with him. I think you'll be okay." Opening the refrigerator, she scanned the shelves.

"He said I would have my own private room."

"Yeah, well, I'm sure he has other intentions," she winked, holding a bowl of strawberries in one hand and shaking a can of whipped cream with the other.

"Whatever!" I rolled my eyes.

After indulging in waffles and deflecting Cindy's inquiry about my night with David, she headed to the gym, and I dressed for work. As I shoved my feet into a pair of three-inch pumps, I dreaded the thought of the next eight hours. Soon I'd be rushing around, choking on second-hand smoke, and taking orders from annoying guests. My thoughts slowly drifted elsewhere.

I pictured myself wearing a comfortable cotton sundress and strolling along the beach barefoot with a frayed straw hat on my head. I'd be inhaling salty sea air and hanging out with cute little sloths, creatures more my speed. I was burned out; I had been burning the candles at both ends.

On my days off, I had started writing again. When I was a young girl, I used to write poems and had even written a few children's books. Short stories that always included animals: dogs, pigs, frogs, birds, you name it. I had come across some of my old writings while packing for my move. Reading them brought me back to my younger days when I had more time to be creative. Maybe if I had pursued my love of writing children's books years ago, I wouldn't have ended up at some dead-end hotel job.

As I made my way toward the Crystal Lounge, dodging convention-of-the-week attendees, I saw Nicole leaning against the bar laughing with the bartender. As I drew near, she caught sight of me, lowering her head. Quickly picking up her drink order, she hurried away, and I wondered what her sudden exit was all about.

After I stashed my handbag inside the employee closet, I was pinning my name tag to my uniform when my supervisor approached me. She stood there, glaring at me with her Sky Royal emblazoned coffee mug in hand, her fingernails thrumming against it.

"Valerie, follow me. I need a word with you, please."

Oh no, this can't be good, I thought.

I followed Natasha into her office and she closed the door behind us.

"So," pursing her lips, she inhaled and let out a long sigh. "What's this I hear about a dinner date at The

Amethyst?" she asked, raising a freshly micro-bladed eyebrow.

Dumb Nicole and her big fat mouth—she needs to lay off the fillers.

"It was my night off and it was only dinner." I shifted uncomfortably in my seat.

"I don't need all the intimate details," she said, waving her hand in front of my face. "I heard enough already."

"Intimate details? Nothing happened."

"You know the policy, right? I assume you read it before you signed it?"

"Yes," I sighed.

"Well, considering this isn't the first time something like this has happened, I'm going to have to adhere to company rules and let you go." Folding her long, licorice-colored fingernails over her hands, she leered at me.

"Not the first time? What are you talking about? Nothing like this has ever happened before."

As she shuffled and reshuffled the papers on her desk, a memory popped into my mind. Last year Cindy had briefly dated a high-roller, a well-known casino guest. She had brought a change of clothes to work, and they went out one night after her shift. I warned her she was taking a risk with the chance of being seen with him at the hotel. But of course, she didn't listen.

When her car wouldn't start that night, I had to drive back to the hotel to pick her up. She wasn't answering my texts, so I had to go inside the hotel to find her. Someone must've seen us and thought we were all together.

"Natasha, wait, I can explain everything," I pleaded.

"Sorry, Valerie, as I said, company rules."

I gazed at Natasha in her tight black dress, with her long, jet black hair, and dark red lipstick. All that was missing was a whip by her side to show her authority.

"But what about tonight? I'm already here, and I—"

"Nicole will cover. It's already taken care of. She can handle it."

That little snitch. That must've been what she was laughing about with the bartender.

"If you have any uniforms at home, please return them tomorrow. However, you won't be able to enter the employee area as you'll be handing over your key card tonight. I'll have someone escort you out."

"Escort me out? My goodness, you act like I've committed a crime." Shaking my head, I couldn't believe what was happening.

I had no idea what I was going to do.

6

David

She said yes. It took a little coaxing on my end, but she finally agreed and obeyed my wishes.

When she called to inform me she had been fired from her job, I was sorry to hear but ecstatic to learn she would be accompanying me on my trip. Now we'll have the chance to become better acquainted, really get to know each other on a deeper level. They say when you travel together, especially with someone new, you learn every little detail about that person. You get to know that person's likes and dislikes, their quirks and behaviors, and the way they handle unexpected situations.

Not that I'm expecting any unexpected situations, but

there could be delays, a change in itinerary, those sorts of things that pop up when you travel. But I'll be sure to have everything planned out, down to the last detail. It's not the way I typically travel, I'll have to admit. I've always been a fly-by-the-seat-of-my-pants kind of guy. However, Val is unique, and this trip will be different, unlike my past travels alone.

Not that I was ever really alone, per se. There's always a woman or two around willing to keep me company. Sure, I've had my temptations as all men have. But I've learned my lesson because temptations have never served me well in the past. I'm not into drama. I have no desire to be tangled in a web of deceit. It never ends well, and quite frankly, I'm tired of bad endings. Things in my life are different now. I'm looking forward to starting anew, beginning a new chapter in my life. I'm not getting any younger. If there's one thing I've learned from past, failed relationships, its control. This time I'll be the one in control of the ending.

A knock on the front door interrupts my thoughts. I'm not expecting anyone.

When I gaze through the peephole, I see her — half-naked, standing on the steps, fiddling with her hair. I open the door.

"David, you're home. Where have you been? You haven't been answering my texts."

Shoving her way past me, she strides into the living room, dumps her overstuffed tote bag on the floor, and proceeds to flop on my couch.

"Kayla, how are you? I haven't seen you in a while."

"I've been sooo busy. Working two jobs is total madness," she says, chomping a wad of gum. She starts blowing pink bubbles, smacking them against her lips. "What have you been up to these days?" Another loud popping sound as she reaches for a magazine on the table.

"I've been busy with things. I'm getting ready to leave town soon."

"You sure travel a lot. Where are you off to now? The jungle again?"

"How'd you guess?"

"So, when do I get to go?" she simpers.

"Kayla, we've already been—."

"I know, I know. But I could sure use a vacation right about now."

"So, what's going on, what do you need?"

"A few photos by the pool. I have a new client requesting a summer vibe look," she says, flipping through the pages.

"Didn't we already take a bunch of pool shots?"

"Uh huh, but that was last year when I was a brunette. They want current. I've lost like fifteen pounds since then." She jumps up from the couch and does a pirouette in her too-tight pink tank top and even tighter white shorts.

"I see that. You look good." I repress a smile.

"Not good enough to take on vacation, though." Crossing her arms, she pouts in disappointment.

"Kayla, come on now. I'm old enough to be your father."

"So, what does that matter? We've been friends forever." Batting her lashes, she makes that little jerking move she does with her head. So full of herself, miss sassy pants. I'm sure her type of attitude is necessary for her line of work—a fine line between cocky and confident.

For the record, I've only known her for two years, and I have to say her feisty demeanor comes through in all her photos. She's lucky to be so photogenic. Most girls would kill to look like her, and most men would kill to be in my position.

But I'm no fool. I've been nothing but professional with Kayla. It's one line I will never cross. She's opened up to me over the years, about her past and her struggles. I've tried helping her many times, tried steering her in the right direction. But she's headstrong. Sadly, she's learning the hard way. At this point, all I can be is a shoulder to lean on and sometimes cry on.

But today, I will do as she asks. Without me, she would never have been hired by the agency. They loved the photos of her the moment they saw her portfolio. They told her the photographer has a real eye and knows what he is doing. Of course, I know what I'm doing, even more so today.

Kayla grabs her bag, I gather my equipment, and we head outside to the pool. She shows me all of her outfits, draping them over the lounge chair. She trusts my choices in swimwear and follows my commands for positions. She says I always know what's best and she's right.

While I adjust the reflector stand, Kayla sashays into the

cabana to change clothes. It's another beautiful spring day in California. The sun shines bright in the clear blue sky, and the colorful flowers surrounding the pool provide the perfect backdrop for a photoshoot.

When the cabana door opens, Kayla struts across the concrete in a pair of high-heeled sandals. She has donned the red string bikini with the short, sheer sarong tied just below her waist.

As I gaze into the lens, Kayla swings her long, wavy hair over her shoulder and thrusts out her hip. Tilting her head to the side, she flashes me a dazzling smile.

Focus, I force myself. *You need to focus.*

7

Valerie

David had insisted I fly to LA that day so we could be on the same flight to Costa Rica. He figured it would be easier on me since it was my first time in Central America. He also didn't want to chance us being separated from each other.

After flying into LAX at ten in the morning, we grabbed a quick bite at the airport and then boarded our flight. We didn't arrive in San Jose until almost eight that night.

There was not much to see in the back of a taxi cab as we made our way to our B&B. Salsa music streamed from the radio, and I had no idea of the meaning of the words they were singing. I hadn't had any time to take a crash course in Spanish. Thankfully David had told me he knew a few phrases, enough of the basics to get around.

On the plane, David had also mentioned he preferred to stay somewhere low key, in the local neighborhoods. Since I had just spent two years being confined to a fancy high-rise hotel, I was open to new experiences.

Thirty minutes later, our taxi turned off the main road down into a long driveway littered with potholes. The sun had set hours ago, and there weren't many street lights in the area. It seemed as if our driver was taking us to the middle of nowhere. David reached over and grabbed my hand, sensing my apprehension.

"You doing okay?" he asked, squeezing my fingers.

"Yeah, it's just so dark, and I have no clue where we are," I replied, gazing out the window toward the inky sky.

When the taxi finally came to a stop, David let go of my hand. He hopped out of the car and went around the back as the driver exited and opened the trunk. I climbed out of the back seat and stood looking all around me, not that I could make out much more than the dense trees and dim lighting outside a few stand-alone structures. The sound of hundreds of buzzing insects filled the evening air.

"Listen to those cicadas," David noted. After paying the driver, David carried our bags as I followed him along a weed-filled walkway. Thick blades of grass poked at my toes, and I wished I hadn't worn sandals on the flight. I should have changed my shoes.

"Welcome to Villa Manuela," a voice said. It belonged to a stocky man who appeared from the ferns.

"Miguel," David announced. "How have you been?"

They shook hands, and then Miguel reached out beside him. "Mi amigo, let me help you with your bags."

"Thank you, my friend," David said, handing him my luggage while keeping his duffle bag strapped to his shoulder.

We followed Miguel down a paved stone walkway with lantern lights lining the path. When we reached a small building, we stood under a bright spotlight above the door. Slipping his hand inside his pocket, Miguel withdrew two keys, each one attached to a small piece of wood with a number painted on it.

"Room number tres y cuatro," he said, dropping a key in each of our hands. "The rooms, they juntos—they join together, but you can lock the door between them." I glanced down to see a red number three key in my palm. *Girl number three, how fitting?* I giggled silently to myself.

David gazed over at me, and for a moment, I thought I had laughed out loud. I was exhausted and needed sleep. I hadn't slept much the night before because I stayed up packing, trying to decide what to take. After a long day of flying and then landing in a strange country, I was ready to fall into bed.

"Breakfast is served between siete y nueve. I wish you both a good night's sleep. See you, mañana, in the morning.

Enjoy your stay, mi amigos." Nodding at me and then David, Miguel turned and walked away, disappearing into the night.

I unlocked the door and entered the room, running my fingers along the wall, searching for a light switch. As the room lit up, I was greeted with a burst of color. The high ceiling gave way to exposed beams painted bright yellow. A wicker bed with matching furniture was also painted yellow. The chair cushions had a green floral design, and the terracotta tiled floor was warm and inviting. Tropical paintings graced the walls, some featuring parrots, others with hummingbirds and flowers. David soon entered behind me.

"You going to be okay in here alone?" he asked, setting my luggage at the foot of the bed.

"I'll be fine. This room is super cute, very colorful. I like it." Smiling, I glided over to a wall where long yellow curtains were hung, touching the floor. Peeking behind them, I saw a huge window. I was eager to see what the view would be in the morning.

"Should I lock the adjoining door or keep it open?"

"Closed but unlocked, please." Unzipping my luggage, I unpacked a few items.

"Okay, get some rest and holler if you need me. See you in the morning for breakfast." As he lingered for a moment unsure of approaching me for either a hug or a kiss goodnight, I glanced over at him.

"Good night," I waved. "Don't let the cicadas bite."

"They don't," he said, "and neither do I." Shaking his head, he closed the door behind him.

After placing my toiletries in the bathroom, I changed into my nightshirt and collapsed into bed. My stomach started growling, and I couldn't wait for breakfast in the morning.

As I started to doze off, I heard something by the door. Not a knock, but a faint scratching sound, a long moment of silence, and then scratching again. Throwing back the covers, my bare feet hitting the tiled floor, I slowly padded over to the adjoining door. When I leaned my ear against the thick slab of wood, I heard nothing.

As I made my way back to bed, the scratching sound began again. I soon realized it was coming from the front door, and my heart rate sped up a bit. I thought about waking David but figured he was off in dreamland.

I slowly made my way over to the front door, placing my hand above the handle, and that's when I heard it—a tiny meow. Cracking open the door, a brown tabby kitty came rushing through and hopped onto the bed. I immediately locked the door behind me and went over to the cat.

"Hello, sweet boy." He came up to me, head butting my arm. I checked him over, making sure he wasn't hurt or injured. Other than being on the skinny side, he appeared to be okay.

"Well, this is a pleasant surprise. I didn't know you were

part of the amenities." He meowed at me as if to say hello and began to purr, rubbing up against me.

I crawled back into bed, laying my head on the pillow. The cat curled up next to me in the crook of my arm, and we both drifted off to sleep.

8

David

When I open my eyes, it's just after seven. Springing out of bed, I am ready to relax and enjoy a week with Val. I wander over to the window, throw back the curtains, and gaze at the lush green mountains in the distance. It's beautiful outside, the sun is shining, and it's a glorious day to be alive.

As I deep breathe through my ten-minute morning yoga routine, I visualize our day— breakfast, a leisurely walk around the grounds, and maybe an early dinner in town.

When I approach the adjoining door to Val's room, I hear the water running. She's up and at 'em—already in the shower. *That's my girl.* After throwing on a T-shirt and cargo shorts, I slide my feet into a pair of flip-flops and head out the door.

I make my way down the pathway through a tropical garden oasis filled with an array of fragrant orchids. When I reach the outdoor seating area, I see the owner behind the bar. With her thick black hair tied back in a ponytail, she's wearing her signature floral apron over her dress. She has a bowl of oranges in front of her and is making freshly squeezed juice for the guests.

"Hola, Manuela," I wave. "¿Como estás?"

"Daveed!" she exclaims, her eyes smiling. "Estoy bien, ¿y tú?"

"Excelente!" I reply. Sneaking behind the bar, I give her a hug.

"¿Qué te gustaría?" she asks, what would I like?

"Dos cafés, por favor," I reply, taking a seat on a bright green bar stool.

"¿Dos?" she questions, a puzzled expression crossing her face. "Two?"

"Para mi amiga." For my friend, I say.

"Sí, sí, la mujer," she winks.

Yes, the woman.

With two hot coffees in hand-painted cups, I stroll back toward my room. As I turn the corner, from a distance, I can see Val through the window. Slowing my pace, I watch as she gets dressed, seemingly not knowing her room faces the garden area. I inch my way closer almost to her door when she turns and looks straight out the window. Her jaw drops as she crosses her arms over her bra-covered chest and ducks from view.

I take a seat on one of the wicker chairs outside her room. Two minutes later, she opens the door, fully dressed, her face slightly flushed.

"Coffee," I say, passing a cup to her.

"I didn't know room service was included." Taking the cup from my hands, she sits down on the chair next to me. "This place looks completely different in the daytime. And I had no idea my window faced a public area."

"Now, you do." Raising the cup to my lips, I take a long sip, savoring the taste.

"This is excellent coffee. I'll have to buy some to take home."

"So, what would you like to do today?"

"Oh, I don't know, I thought you had to work?"

"Not today. We're only staying here another night before we fly to a different location."

"Okay, whatever you say. This whole trip slash vacation is your deal. I'm just tagging along for the ride."

Whatever I say is right. She sure is learning quickly. I like that. This obedience is something I could definitely get used to.

———

At breakfast, she orders an omelette con queso, and I have my favorite dish, huevos rancheros. Between bites, we make small talk until I purposely direct the conversation to discuss news and current events. It's my way of gauging her knowledge and interest in what's happening in the world. If a woman can carry a conversation with me and complete more than two sentences, it tells me I have found someone I can work with.

Manuela comes over to top off our coffees with a cat trailing behind her.

"Here kitty, kitty," Val says in a high-pitched voice. She leans over in her chair to pet the furry little creature. "He slept with me last night."

"Who did? The cat?" A twinge of jealousy stirs inside me.

"Yeah, it was around midnight when I heard a scratching at the door. At first, I didn't know what it was, and then I heard a meow. As soon as I opened the door, he ran inside as if he owned the place. He hopped up onto the bed and slept right beside me."

"You shouldn't be opening the door at night," I say, my voice stern. "Not here or anywhere else, for that matter, but especially not here," I emphasize. Holding her gaze, I wait for a reply.

"Sorry, but he wanted to come in." She continues to pet him, stroking his back. "Besides, who could say no to this cute little guy?" She flashes me a set of puppy dog eyes.

"Next time, it might not be a cute little guy. It might be a big, mean old man holding a machete." Raising my arm, I pretend to hold a long knife in my hand and slash the air.

She stares at me with fear in her eyes. "Then what would you have done?" I ask, holding her gaze.

Silence. Crickets. She doesn't know what to say.

"I'm sorry," she finally mutters, glancing down at the feline. "I guess I cave when it comes to animals, especially cats."

Please don't tell me she's one of those crazy cat ladies. I'm allergic to them both: cats and crazy women.

After breakfast, we walk the grounds, not a word out of Val's mouth as she takes in the sights. I imagine she's still upset because I semi-scolded her for being so naïve about her midnight visitor. Did she momentarily forget she's in a foreign country?

I force myself to give her a pass; she clearly didn't know any better. At least now, I know one of her weaknesses—cute fuzzy animals. I wonder if she's the type to dress them up in absurd little outfits. You see it everywhere in LA. Mini-Poodles and Pomeranians dressed in pink tutus with their toenails painted to match. If they're not being toted around in some overpriced designer bag, they're being pushed in a baby stroller. Do they have any idea how ridiculous they look? There are children in this world who don't have anywhere near the wardrobes those spoiled doggies possess. Women down here in this country carry their children in their arms. They don't have the luxury of a stroller.

Most people don't know how good they have it until they travel outside their comfort zone. Sadly, many turn a blind eye, unable to face the harsh realities of the real world. Some are too caught up with the meaningless stuff being shoved in their faces daily. 'Buy this,' 'buy that'… it's nothing but a constant stream of advertising to spend, spend, spend. For what? To go broke? To max out their credit cards trying to keep up with the latest trends.

It doesn't make an ounce of sense to me. Not when there are hundreds and thousands of people in dire need of the very basics, food, clothing, and shelter.

Traveling has opened my eyes to many things. It has opened my eyes to the real world, the raw, untouched, and untold world where many people live with next to nothing. Every day they rise with smiles on their faces, attend to the tasks at hand, work hard to make a dollar, and repeat the sequence the next day for their entire lives.

As I gaze over at Val, she's glistening. I watch as she wipes dots of perspiration from her forehead. It is eighty-nine degrees today with a hundred percent humidity. It's different from the dry desert heat she's used to. She tugs at the front of her T-shirt, pulling it away from her chest as it sticks to her skin.

"Maybe you should've worn a sundress," I suggest. "You might have been cooler."

"Yeah, I know. I need to iron a few things, but there's no iron in the room."

"What do you say we stop at the bar before we head back to the room? Manuela makes a tasty batido."

"What's a batido?"

"A fruit smoothie with milk."

"Sounds good right about now."

As we sit sipping our smoothies, I study Val's face. She looks different without all the heavy makeup she usually wears. With her lips glossed a shade of coral, and her hair pulled up into a high ponytail, she looks much younger.

"What are you staring at?" She fidgets uncomfortably.

"You," I reply, reaching for her drink. Sliding it in front of me, I take a long sip from the straw. Her forehead wrinkles as she narrows her eyes.

"Is there a problem?" I ask.

"You just drank from my straw."

"Are you afraid I'll catch something?"

"No." She giggles, rolling her eyes. "There's nothing to catch from me."

"Then why the worried look? I don't have cooties; I just wanted a little taste." I slide the drink back toward her. "I should have ordered the pineapple instead of the papaya. I like yours better."

I lean back and watch as a shiny violet hummingbird hovers near a brilliant red heliconia. Poking its long needle-like beak into the flower, it flutters its wings, drinking and swallowing the sweet nectar. I glance over at Val and see that she's looking at the bird as well.

As I turn my head back to the tiny bird, it flies away as another appears. This one colored bright blue and green zooms in and drinks from the same flower. The tiny little hummingbirds aren't afraid to share, and I wonder for a moment if Val gets the message. It's okay to share things with someone you love. It's called trust. You need to have faith in each other.

Could Val be someone I love? Someone I can trust? Someone to have faith in?

Only time will tell...

9

Valerie

"So, what did you want to be when you grew up?" David asked, over our second glass of sangria. "Surely it wasn't a Vegas cocktail waitress."

"No, definitely not," I said, licking the sweet wine from my lips. "Cheers to me losing my job," I raised the glass in front of me.

"Cheers!" he replied. "You've been freed from a life of polyester."

We laughed as we clinked glasses over a flickering candle between us.

"Seriously, what did you dream about when you were young? How did you picture your life?"

"Well," taking another sip, I swallowed. "I dreamed about writing children's books... books that would include animals."

"That makes sense, seeing how you bonded with Mr. Tiger kitty last night."

"And I'd love to travel the world."

"Where would you start?"

"Oh, maybe a train ride through Europe or take an African safari."

"Adventurous, I like that in a woman."

"Speaking of women, care to share a little bit about your past, your marriages?"

"Not particularly," he said, clearing his throat.

The waitress appeared at the table with our dinner at just the right moment. David had ordered the olla de carne and I, the ceviche with a side of patacones.

"I guess I'm just curious why they didn't work out," I uttered. Reaching into the dish, I grabbed a patacon and munched on it.

"One word," he replied, chewing a piece of beef, "jealous."

"Jealous? Of what?"

"I don't know. I think they lacked confidence."

"Both of them? I find that kind of hard to believe... unless you have a certain type."

"I don't really have a type. Perhaps they couldn't handle a man like me."

"What do you mean?" I seized another patacon. "A man

like what?"

"I'm outgoing, adventurous. I like to experience new things. And I travel a great deal for work."

"And they couldn't handle that?"

"Apparently not, sometimes my actions would be mistaken for flirting. Not on my part, mind you, but there were times when my actions were misconstrued."

"Misconstrued?"

"Yes, women would hit on me when I was just being friendly."

"Hmm… you know what they say—it takes two to tango."

"And I only tango with one woman at a time."

Reaching for the glass pitcher of sangria, he poured us another round, and then lowered his head, taking bite after bite of his food.

"You know, I really don't want to talk about my past. The past is the past and that's where it belongs. I want to focus on the here and now, the present moment, with you. It's all we have."

"Okay, but how are we supposed to get to know each other?"

"I get it. You women need to know everything about everything, all the tiny details. It's part of your DNA."

"You say it like it's a bad thing."

"No, it's not bad, but everything has its place. For instance, if I bring home the bacon and you fry it, why does there have to be fifty questions about it? Can't you just cook the bacon so we can enjoy it together? I do my part, and you do yours. That sort of thing."

"So basically, correct me if I'm wrong, what you're saying is you want a fifty-fifty relationship, give and take."

"Yes."

"And you've never had that before?"

"Most started out that way. Both parties are on their best behavior in the beginning. But then over time, little grievances build up, and things go sideways, or south in my case."

"How long did they last?"

"Around seven years each," he stabbed at the beef, setting the fork aside.

"Ahh, the seven-year itch."

"I don't buy into that notion. It is what it is, and it is what it was."

He seemed slightly irritated, and I didn't want to push the issue. I didn't want to come across as a nag, which would surely dishearten him. Besides, who was I to judge? I know relationships can be tough; mine had failed.

The lights dimmed and the salsa music grew louder. David started moving to the rhythm, and my mind drifted back to my younger days when I had spent weekends dancing the night away.

At one point, I had come close to marrying Joey, my high school sweetheart. That was before he started drinking heavily and subsequently cheating on me. I've had my guard up ever since, not being able to trust a man or men in general. And then moving to Vegas didn't help matters. If anything, it had only made things worse. The thought of meeting a decent man only existed in my dreams.

Years ago, I kept having the same recurring dream. I was a passenger in a car being driven by an older, dark-haired man. The dream was just one scene, a continual road trip. I was very comfortable with the man in my dreams as we traveled along winding roads in deep conversation.

Every so often, my dream man would take his eyes off the road, glance over at me with a smile, and reach for my hand.

"Would you like to dance?" I heard a voice speak in the distance.

"Val! Earth to Val."

Upon hearing my name, I turned and saw David smiling at me, his hand outstretched, reaching toward mine.

My heart skipped a beat—his face. I had seen it before, the man in my dreams—the dark-haired, slightly older gentleman. *Oh my goodness, could it be? Could I have conjured up David from my dreams?*

"Is everything okay?" he asked, his head tilted to the side.

I just sat there staring at him, studying him.

"Why the strange look? I only asked if you wanted to dance."

"Yeah, sure, why not," I slowly rose from the chair, my legs unsteady beneath me after three glasses of sangria.

Lacing his fingers through mine, he led me to the small

dance floor as the music changed. The sound of the conga drums faded away, replaced by a different, slower-paced tempo.

David pulled me close, one hand supporting my back and the other holding my hand while steadying my arm. I followed his lead. We began swaying side to side, cheek to cheek, being careful not to step on each other's toes. The temperature between us soon heated up as he spun me around and dipped me to the side, hovering over me with a penetrating gaze.

"Do you know what they call this type of dancing?" he asked.

"Not sure, exactly," I said, maneuvering to the left. "You're mixing steps from several styles of dance."

"I do like to mix it up a bit. Keep things fresh."

"It feels like you're making it up as you go along." My head was spinning from too many twirls, coupled with too much sangria.

"I'm going to call this one the hummingbird tango," he said, gazing deep into my eyes. "I hope you remember what I said earlier. It's imperative."

"Oh, what was that?"

He pulled me in closer, his lips trailing along my neck as he whispered in my ear. "I only tango with one woman."

10

David

Last night was fun with a capital F. The most fun I've had in a long time. I am on my best behavior this time around. I'll need to keep the alcohol flowing with this one; she seems to open up more and relax when she's had a cocktail or two. I need someone who can loosen up, someone who can go with the flow—my flow. I can't handle another uptight woman. They've never been my style anyway.

I have to say, though, I'm going to need to take her shopping. Her taste in lingerie differs from mine. I like things much more form-fitting and revealing. Let's just say less cotton and more spandex.

She must realize men are visual creatures. At least the

men I know. Sure we let our eyes linger when an attractive woman passes by, even when we're with you. We're not dead, for heaven's sake, we have testosterone running through our veins—twenty-four-seven.

But when a woman's not dressed the way we prefer, when they're too covered up, we have to imagine what they'd look like less covered up. It's more work on our part, and I have enough on my plate right now. I need a woman who will wear the clothes I buy her, not stick them in the back of her closet as if ashamed to own them.

Take last night, for example, the two good-looking women who were dining next to us at the restaurant. The blonde to our left, on vacation with her boyfriend. The brunette to our right, having dinner with her husband. Both were dressed in provocative attire—outfits more to my liking.

But you didn't notice me leering at them. No, not this time, I made sure of it. I had to sneak a peek here and there when you weren't looking. One of those times was when you were devouring your dish of patacones. It was quite a generous portion they gave you, and it's a good thing I shared with you. You'll need to go easy on the fried food if you are going to be with a man like me. Fried food is a quick way to pack on extra pounds. And I like my women curvy, not plump. You'll need to know and remember that detail.

I suppose I could pay for a personal trainer if you go beyond my desired weight range. But that's just another expense I don't need right now. I could be your personal trainer if I had to. I would work those extra pounds off you —free of charge.

But I'm getting ahead of myself. You still have curves in all the right places. We just have to make sure we keep them where they belong.

I mean let's be honest; I'm not going to lie. When we met, you were a cocktail waitress. You captured my attention. That little uniform of yours fitted you perfectly, showing off your shapely body. When you leaned over, setting the glass on the table, you wouldn't want to know what I was thinking. If you did, you probably would've reached out and slapped me across the face.

But when my eyes met yours, I could tell you were different, unlike the others. The other gals are there to work what they got, shake their little tail feathers in hopes of landing a rich guy to whisk them away in some fairytale romance. But I don't believe in fairy tales.

When I first saw you, I could tell you were there to work and earn a living. You kept things professional when we spoke. Then over time, you opened up a little. Not too much, but enough to share your hopes and dreams. Dreams you're determined to fulfill on your own.

Sometimes, though, it's not that easy. In some instances, we could all use a little help. That's where I come in. I like to help. I like to fix things. I'm really good at fixing things. You'll see. Time will tell, but time is ticking away. I have to make sure we're on the same timeframe.

Speaking of time, we'll be leaving shortly for our next destination. I hope you like what I have in store for you. Do you like surprises? On second thought, you don't strike me as the type of woman who does. You're probably more organized and would rather be prepared and ready for things ahead of time. Am I right?

I stroll over by your window and peek into your room. I can see you packing right now, preparing to head out on our next adventure. I do hope you'll be okay with the small island hopper plane. I hope you don't scream and squirm in your seat like the last one did when we landed on the tiny airstrip.

I told her to remain calm and to hold onto my hand as the plane dipped toward the sea. I told her not to worry and not to be scared that the pilot had flown the route a thousand times and that he could land the plane with his eyes closed. But she refused to listen. She just kept screaming and crying; she lost all control. I don't like it when things are out of control. I don't like it when women don't comply with my wishes.

She didn't obey me that day. Needless to say, it didn't end well.

Valerie

The next morning I had woken up to David's arm wrapped around my waist. Prying myself from his grip, I quietly dressed and crept out of the room to fetch some coffee. We had a plane to catch and couldn't be late since it was the only flight available that day.

Once we arrived at the airport, we picked up our tickets and hopped on a shuttle bus that drove us to the tarmac. We boarded a small airplane, and less than an hour later landed along the Caribbean Sea.

When our taxi pulled up to The Green Tree House, I was thrilled to see it was located by the ocean. With its open-air wooden houses nestled in the trees, we were steps away from the white sand beach.

We were greeted by a young tanned and toned couple who managed the ecolodge. They informed us of the yoga classes, water sports, and guided tours around the area. David had mentioned he wanted to go zip-lining, but the excitement quickly faded from his eyes when I shared my great fear of heights.

"We may have to change rooms then?" he said, turning to me.

"Why?"

"You'll see."

I cautiously followed David over a sloped wooden suspension bridge that led to our room—the treehouse room. As the walkway swayed and bounced under my feet, I was thankful it was only about fifty feet long and ten feet high.

Inside the room, massive tree trunks rose up from the floor. Off to the right was a small kitchenette and to the left, a king-sized bed with a white mosquito net draped above it. The best feature of the treehouse was the wrap-around deck with a panoramic view of the ocean. David slid one of the windows open, and we listened to the sound of the crashing waves.

"So, what do you think?" he asked, a wide smile appearing on his face.

"This is a really cool place. I've never been anywhere like it."

"I apologize for the room; I had no idea you were afraid of heights. Do you want me to see if there's a ground level room available?"

"No, it's fine; we're here now."

"Okay, well, you take the bed and I'll take the hammock out on the deck."

"You don't have to."

"I have no problem sleeping out there. I can't remember the last time I slept in one."

"But the mosquitoes will eat you alive."

"Well, in that case, maybe that tiny couch turns into a bed," he said, pointing to the love seat in the middle of the room. "I can sleep there."

Fixing his gaze on me, I could tell what he was thinking. From the look in his eyes, he was thinking of the previous night.

"Although we seemed to do okay last night sharing a bed," his eyes wandering over to the king-sized bed. "I think there's enough room for both of us."

I nodded slowly, feeling my face flush. I walked over to the window and looked out through the trees to the blue ocean waters. As a gentle breeze blew through my hair, I breathed deeply, filling my lungs with the fresh sea air.

Moments later, I felt David approach me from behind. With his hands running over my shoulders and down my back, he then wrapped his arms around my waist, whispering in my ear.

"We have five nights here before we head back home. Let's make the most of it."

It was a relaxing week and I spent every day lounging on the beach. David worked from the room in the mornings, making phone calls and typing on his laptop. He would join me for lunch and we'd hang out for a few hours before dinner. We did yoga, went horseback riding, and hiked to see the waterfalls, traversing though the rainforest.

On our last night, David had a surprise for me. We went out to eat at a romantic beachfront restaurant, and he ordered a bottle of champagne.

"What are we celebrating?" I asked.

"I want you to know that I've had one of the best weeks I've ever had. I like being with you, our conversation flows, and I'm comfortable around you." He took a quick sip of his drink, studying me. "I was thinking since you lost your job and mentioned you were interested in moving to California…" his voice trailed off.

I leaned in, reaching for my champagne and took a long sip.

"As I was saying, I think you should move. You should come live with me."

Gripping the glass, I took another sip and swallowed. "You can't be serious?"

"Why not? What do we have to lose? If you don't like it, you can always move back."

"But we hardly know each other."

"I'd say we've gotten to know each other pretty well over the past week," he winked.

The tiny alarm bell inside me was quelled with my overwhelming attraction to him. I questioned how I could have felt so strongly for someone so soon. I was always one to follow my gut feelings, and at that very moment, my stomach was sending me mixed messages. Was it nerves? Was it butterflies from the crush I had developed on him? Or was it a warning?

The champagne wasn't helping matters; it was clouding my thoughts. My head was telling me to go slow but my heart was telling me otherwise. I had developed genuine feelings for him.

"What do you say, Val?"

"I appreciate the offer but wasn't expecting it."

"I'll sweeten the deal and throw in a bonus."

"Oh," I giggled. "A bonus, huh?

"Sure. Moving in with me will include frequent free trips to Costa Rica."

"You don't say."

"If everything works out the way I hope it will, maybe someday we'll live here."

"Here, in Costa Rica?" I glanced up and all around. "I'd say that's getting a little ahead of yourself."

"It's something I've been planning for a while now. But

I'm willing to take baby steps with you if that's what you need."

Leaning back in my chair, I took in my surroundings while pondering David's offer. I wasn't happy living in Vegas and had just been fired partly because of him. But it wasn't his entire fault; it was mine for accepting his invitation to dinner. And then there was Nicole with her big mouth ratting on me. I figured I could find another job, maybe waitressing or bartending in California. I couldn't deny that the trips to Costa Rica sounded inviting. However, Costa Rica was somewhat different from the Caribbean Islands I had visited. While it was still a tropical destination, it seemed rougher around the edges.

When the bubbly blonde waitress set our dessert on the table, Cindy's face popped into my mind. I couldn't desert my roommate on a whim. We were only able to afford our rental house with both of our incomes. I couldn't just up and leave her because I met someone. Although it was something she would do to me, being the carefree party girl that she was. But it wasn't something I could do; it wasn't my style to leave someone in a lurch.

"Care for a bite?" David asked, holding out a forkful of cream-topped white cake.

I eagerly took a bite as he slid the fork from my mouth. "Wow, that's yummy," I said, over a mouthful of sweet milky sponge cake.

"Tres leches, it's my second favorite dessert after flan," he said, quickly scooping up two forkfuls himself.

After dinner, we strolled barefoot, hand-in-hand, along the shore. White string lights and hanging lanterns illuminated the trees, lighting our path. As we walked a bit farther, David paused for a moment and tilted his head back.

"Look at all the stars."

I gazed up at the midnight sky, the water gently lapping around our feet, our toes sinking in the sand.

"Quick, make a wish."

"A wish?"

"Yes, right there, a shooting star," he pointed above, his finger gliding to the right.

"Are you sure?" I searched the sky, trying to see what had aroused his attention. "Maybe it was a satellite or something?"

"No, it was a shooting star; I'm sure of it." He turned to me, cupping my chin in his hand. "Care to know what I wished for?" he asked, staring into my eyes.

12

David

As I walk around the spare room, making sure everything's in order, I find myself singing the song, 'When You Wish Upon a Star.' Trailing my fingers along the glossy black desk, I picture Val sitting here writing her books. She will be happy doing what she has always wanted to do, and I will provide for her—a picture perfect life, *our* picture perfect life.

Some women enjoy being kept by a man, as long as they're being taken care of. My Val will make me her king, and I will make her my queen. I will promise to give her anything her little heart desires, within limits, of course, as long as she behaves and obeys, as long as she complies with the rules. My rules. Without rules, there is chaos. And I don't do well in chaos.

I've cleaned out the closet, removing any and all traces of my collections. If she were to stumble upon them without my knowledge, she might become alarmed. It's not something you spring on someone without a full explanation.

For now, however, the closet only contains a few little outfits I've carefully selected for her. As I run my hand over the lacy garments dangling from the hangers, I close my eyes momentarily, picturing her in them. Most are her size, as I had sneaked a peek at her clothing tags while on vacation. But some of them are a size smaller. As I mentioned before, she could benefit from a few form-fitting ensembles. My motto has always been if you've got it, flaunt it. But she'll only be flaunting it for me, no one else. And only in the privacy of our home, *my* home.

Speaking of homes, how coincidental was it that her former coworker Nicole needed a place to live? Apparently the house Nicole was renting had been sold, and she only had a month to find other living quarters. Cindy offered Nicole the extra bedroom at their home, which in turn made it much easier for Val to move out. Yes, the stars are aligning for me. It's about time as I've certainly paid my dues.

Rather, I've paid more than my dues. I've supported two wives, giving them everything they asked for in return for so little. I bought them cars, homes, and one of them, a complete head-to-toe makeover. One plastic surgery procedure had led to another and another, and soon she became addicted. She never seemed to be happy with herself. Nothing was ever good enough for her. I suppose this town contributed to her addiction. She never felt comfortable around me when we were out and about. She always acted extremely insecure, always accusing me of cheating on her.

I hope I'm doing the right thing this time. I hope I'm not corrupting an innocent young woman. Val seems so squeaky clean in comparison to the others. On the other hand, however, she also appears strong willed. She has a burning desire to do things on her own. That's one of the reasons I chose her.

Sure, I could've chosen Cindy or Nicole, the two party girls. I've seen them both before, studying them from afar, watching their maneuvers as they flirted with the hotel guests. But I know their type. I know it all too well. They are easily distracted and tend to engage in the silly surface drama.

I'm at a point in my life whereby I cannot tolerate any distractions. I need to focus on my plan one hundred percent. This time around, I need a solid agreement from a woman who wants to go the distance—a woman who knows the genuine meaning of commitment.

I make my way into the kitchen and over to the counter to uncork a bottle of Merlot. As I retrieve a stemmed glass from the cabinet, I think back to my first dinner with Val.

She had ordered white wine, Pinot Grigio, if I recall. If she's to be with a man like me, she's going to have to ditch the white and switch to red. She'll need to learn that red wine has higher levels of antioxidants. If you're going to drink wine, red is the only way to go.

With the glass in hand, I take a seat on the couch and flip open my laptop. After taking a long sip of my wine, I log into my favorite website. I check to see who's online, if I have any new messages and if anyone's interested in what I'm offering. I see a few familiar faces and reply to three messages. Other than that, nothing new has caught my eye.

Reaching for my glass, I swirl the liquid, wondering if I'll be able to check in as much as I do after Val arrives. I still haven't figured out how I'm going to go about introducing her to my world. Will it be something she'll understand? Something she'll accept? Or will it be something that will send her running for the hills?

13

Valerie

The minute I returned home, Cindy was all over me asking a million and one questions.

"So, how did it go? Tell me all about it." She was jumping up and down like a kid in a candy shop.

"It went really well. We had a nice week together. I was pleasantly surprised by how great a travel partner he is. It's been so long since I've traveled with someone."

"You have a killer tan," she said, eyeing me up and down. "What did you guys do all week?"

"Oh, a bunch of activities, David has a ton of energy, much more than I do."

"When are you going to see him again?"

"You're not going to believe this," I paused, biting on my lower lip. "But he asked me to move in with him."

"Get out of here! Are you serious?"

"Yeah, I was speechless. It kinda came out of nowhere. But I—"

"But you like him, right? Of course, you do, I can see it written all over your face. Do you feel comfortable enough with him to move into his house?"

"I do. It's weird because we had an instant connection."

"Well, the timing is right if you're going to take the plunge. With Nicole losing her house and all, she needs another place to live. I figured you'd be okay with it when I offered her the extra room."

"Yeah, thanks for sending me the text. I appreciate the heads up."

For a moment, I thought of telling Cindy my suspicions about Nicole. About her maybe having something to do with getting me fired. But I didn't want to spoil the mood or cause any drama. Besides, things always turn out the way they are supposed to.

"So when do you leave?"

"He wants me to move in as soon as possible. And I need to find a job, so I'll be packing my belongings and leaving this week."

"Who would've thought my little Val would be scooped up from the trenches of the Vegas strip."

"Yeah, well, if it doesn't work out, I don't know what I'll

do. I guess I could always come back here… although it's not my ideal preference."

"I know, but Nicole and I will be here slinging drinks as usual. And we'll always have room for you."

"Thanks, Cindy, I really appreciate it. It means a lot to me."

She reached out and gave me a hug.

Lugging my suitcase down the hall, I quickly unpacked and did a couple loads of laundry. I began cleaning out my closet, packing most of my things into my luggage. I just needed to pick up a few more boxes to pack the rest of my belongings. I didn't have much since I had downsized upon moving to Vegas. At that point, my entire life fit into ten boxes.

Cindy came waltzing into my room, a bottle of Prosecco in one hand, and two wine glasses in the other. Setting them down on the dresser, she poured us a drink.

"A toast to you and your new man," she said, handing me a glass. "I wish you all the best, my friend."

"Thanks." I smiled, raising my glass to her while sitting on the floor in the middle of the room.

"You are going to keep in touch, right?"

"Of course, I am. I don't know anyone in California except David."

"I'm sure you'll make some new friends there."

"Maybe so, but it might take me a while. Between David and finding a new job, I'll probably be pretty busy."

Cindy sat down next to me and started helping me pack.

"Maybe I can come out and visit you? It's been years since I was in LA. I have a few vacation days I need to use before I lose them."

"That would be great. I'm sure David wouldn't mind, and he has a spare room, plus he's an easy-going guy."

"Yeah, if his personality matches his fine looks, I'd say you did good girl." Leaning into me, she elbowed my side.

"I just hope I'm doing the right thing. Everything has happened so quickly."

"I'll have to say it's definitely out of your character. It's not something someone like you would do."

"What's that supposed to mean?" I took another sip of wine.

"I don't know. I guess it's something I figured Nicole would do, but not you."

There was her name again, Nicole. I suppose I'd better get used to it since she'd be moving in and basically taking my place. She was a nice enough person, but sometimes hard to read.

"So when is Nicole moving in?"

"Next week. Maybe we should have a little party and give you a send-off."

"That sounds good."

Cindy stood up and reached for the bottle, refilling her glass and then turning to me.

"No thanks," I placed my hand over the top of the glass. "I need to stop at one. I drank way too much alcohol over the past few weeks."

"Okay, that just means more vino for me." Flipping her hair, she turned and strutted out of the room.

I picked up my laptop and sat on my bed. I hadn't done much research on David aside from checking out his website and photos. For the next two hours, I googled his name, seeing if I could dig up any dirt on him, making sure he was the man he said he was and to give me some peace of mind.

I didn't find much information other than a few old addresses and a couple of defunct websites. But my main concern was finding his ex-wives. Who says 'I do' twice to two different women? I would think after the first time it loses its effect. It ruins the whole meaning of 'to have and to hold—till death do us part.'

Unless. No. Wait a minute. He didn't say he was divorced. Could he be widowed? I couldn't believe I had never thought of it until that moment. *What if one of his wives or both of them were dead?*

Goosebumps dimpled my arms and my stomach twisted and turned. I quickly began searching the addresses, hoping to connect him to the names of his ex-wives. They had to share an address, right? I had to find out if they were still alive.

I first came across a woman named Susan who was linked to him via one of those background information sites. As I clicked on her photo to enlarge it, my computer froze and then crashed, flashing me the blue screen of death.

David

Val is due to arrive at any moment. I gaze out the window, glance down the street, and watch for her silver Jeep. I'm not sure if I should break the news to her right away or wait a day or two. I didn't expect my plans to change so quickly. I thought we would have more time here in California. But it looks as if things are progressing more rapidly and I'm going to have to make the move sooner than I had anticipated.

Perhaps we'll order a take-out meal tonight. We'll share a bottle of wine, cuddle on the couch, and watch a romantic movie together, a chick flick. I'm not a fan of them, but I can suck it up for a night—anything for my Val. That will put her in the mood and relax her a bit. Maybe then I can tell her what she needs to know.

She must have texted me at least twenty times over the past two days, asking me all sorts of questions. For a moment, I thought she was getting cold feet. I thought she was going to back out of our plan. That wouldn't have been good. It would've set me back. I'm so glad I was able to alleviate her worries and put her mind at ease. It's what I do. I'm a master at providing relief.

Thirty minutes later there's a knock on my door. I waltz over to the foyer and turn the handle.

"There's my girl." I flash a genuine smile. "No turning back now," I reach out and embrace her.

"Here I am. I made it. My whole life packed in the back of my Jeep." She looks at me as if she's about to be sick.

"Why don't you park in the garage and bring in the items you'll need for the night. We can unpack the rest of your belongings in the morning."

"Okay."

"I was thinking about ordering take-out food. Do you prefer Chinese or Italian?"

"A pizza would taste good right about now. It's Friday night, after all."

"Is pizza some sort of tradition?" I don't quite understand her meaning.

"Yeah, we always order pizza on Fridays."

"Then a pizza it is," I say with a hesitant breath.

Val walks back to her vehicle and I slide my phone from my pocket. I order a thin crust, veggie pizza. I can't handle heavy cheese and thick bread; it's too much. I don't want to wake up all bloated in the morning. In my book, pizza should only be eaten on special occasions. Although today could probably count as one of those occasions.

I'll let it go this time because we're celebrating. But I will not allow this habit to become a tradition... on Fridays or any other night.

After polishing off three slices of pizza each, we sit on the couch next to each other. I hand Val the remote while I pour us second glasses of wine.

"Pick whatever movie you want to watch. I'm open to anything."

"I love mysteries and old-fashioned psychological thrillers. You know, the ones that make you think," she replies.

I take a sip of wine, holding her gaze, wondering if she can sense my thoughts.

"How about you?" She reaches for her glass. "What's your favorite movie genre?"

"I like a good action-adventure."

Clicking through the remote, she finds her thriller, and I

curl up next to her, putting my arm around her shoulder. Leaning in, I kiss her softly on the cheek and then settle back to enjoy the show.

After an hour, she starts nodding off and misses the end of the movie. Somehow I have the feeling she's seen it before. I gently nudge her, wake her from her slumber and help her to bed, calling it a night.

The next morning I let her sleep in as I mosey into the kitchen to make breakfast. A half-hour later, I hear footsteps padding down the hallway. She soon appears, standing at the edge of the counter rubbing her eyes.

"It smells wonderful in here," she yawns, stretching her arms.

"Good morning. Care for some coffee?"

"Yes, please."

I pour her a steaming cup, placing it on the counter.

"Thanks." Wrapping her hands around the mug, she takes a long sip.

"How about a spinach omelette to go with that?"

"Okay, thank you." She slides onto the barstool and watches me as I maneuver around the kitchen dressed in my boxers.

"So, what's on the agenda today?" she asks.

"I have a few phone calls to make after breakfast. After

that, I'm free. I thought we could take a bike ride down to the beach. I need to burn off that pizza from last night."

"Sounds like a plan; I need to stretch. My back is a little sore from yesterday… from driving all day."

I think about breaking the news to her over breakfast but decide to wait and save it for later. There's no use throwing a curveball at her so early in the morning.

I put on a T-shirt and sweatpants and go downstairs to check the air in the bike tires. Val offers to do the dishes and puts everything away. It's nice to see her stepping up without me having to ask her. It's been less than twenty-four hours and she already seems to feel at home. Too bad we won't be spending much time here together. Sometimes that is the way things go. Everything happens for a reason, they say.

We pedal our way down to the beach and stop, parking our bikes. As we stroll along the boardwalk, I eye an empty bench. Taking her hand, I guide her over to it and sit down beside her. I figure there's no perfect time to break the news to her.

I gather my thoughts but they're interrupted as her phone starts ringing. I watch as she furiously digs through her purse.

"Hello," she says. Then, "I'm sorry. I totally forgot. I know, I know, I meant to. We had dinner, and then I fell asleep. Yeah, I'm okay. Sorry to make you worry. Are you okay? Is everything okay there? Right now? We're at the beach. Yes, I will. I promise I will. Okay. Talk to you later."

"What was that all about?" I ask, a bit concerned.

"Cindy. I forgot to call her when I arrived last night. She was worried about me."

"Sounds like she's looking out for you."

"Yeah, she's a good friend."

A good friend with bad timing, I think to myself.

15

Valerie

One morning I woke up to a note on the nightstand. It read, 'gone to get groceries; be back soon.' David had been leaving me all kinds of memos. Some were love notes and others were reminders and instructions.

The day before, it was 'don't forget to unplug the toaster after you use it' and the previous week, 'turn off the lights when you leave the room and don't use the clothes dryer for more than thirty minutes.' At times I felt like a child being chastised for every move I made.

But then he had left a note on my desk that read, 'this desk belongs to a best-selling author.' I thought it was sweet the way he supported my dreams. He encouraged me to write every day and even bought me a brand new computer. He said he wanted nothing but the best for me, or so it seemed.

After rushing into things so quickly, I told him I needed to take a few steps back, that I was someone who needed my own space. He respected my wishes and was okay with me staying in his spare room. Of course, there were times in the middle of the night when he would sneak in and slide under the covers with me.

When I went to the kitchen to grab a glass of water that morning, I noticed David's keys on the counter. *That's strange,* I thought to myself as I walked downstairs and headed toward the garage. I opened the door and my jeep was gone. He had taken my vehicle to buy groceries. I was a bit taken back at first but then figured he had a good reason. Maybe he was having car trouble.

I was about to walk back upstairs and take a shower when the doorbell rang. Still dressed in my pajamas, I was hesitant to open the door. When I looked through the peephole, I saw a heavily made-up young woman standing there. My first thought was maybe she was at the wrong house.

As I opened the door, she barged right in and stood in the foyer.

"Is David here?" she asked, chewing a piece of gum and gazing over my shoulder.

"Uh, no, he's not. He should be back shortly, though." A handful of questions flashed through my mind.

Glaring at me, she twirled a long strand of hair. "And who are you?"

"I'm Valerie, and you are?"

"Kayla," she replied, eyeing me up and down through her inch-long lashes. "David has something of mine I need to pick up."

"I'll let him know you stopped by."

"He has my number. Tell him to call me."

"Okay then."

She spun around and headed back out the door. In her tiny tank top and short shorts, I watched as she turned the sidewalk into a catwalk, her long blonde ponytail bouncing behind her.

What on earth have I stepped into? I had to shake the unpleasant thoughts that entered my mind. She acted as if she knew him well and I wondered how well. I headed down the hallway and into the bathroom. I needed a long, hot shower to wash away my unconfirmed thoughts.

When David came home, it was lunchtime, and at that point, he had been gone for nearly four hours.

"Hi," he leaned in, kissing me on the cheek. "I'm going to make a salad. Care to share?"

"Yeah, sounds healthy." Gazing at him, I noticed his face was flushed. He didn't make much eye contact as he started chopping vegetables.

"What have you been doing this morning? Have you been writing?"

"No, not yet, I'm a little slow getting started today."

"Well, don't let me interfere. After lunch, I need to run back out."

I couldn't imagine why he would have to leave so soon when he had just returned. And prior thoughts were creeping their way back into my mind.

"Someone stopped by earlier looking for you."

"Oh, who?"

"Kayla."

"She's my neighbor."

"She said you have something of hers she needed to pick up."

"I do. Her photos."

"Photos? Of her?"

"I took some photos of her for her portfolio. She's a model."

"Oh, I see."

"I could take some of you if you'd like."

"But I'm not a model."

"But you could be." He glanced up from the cutting board covered with diced tomatoes and cucumbers.

"Nice try."

"You're not upset, are you?"

"No, no I'm not upset. It's just the way she burst in here like she owned the place."

"That's Kayla," he let out a laugh, "that's how she is."

"So she's been here before."

"Well, yeah, you know I'm a photographer, right. I may be an amateur, but still…"

"What else do you do with her?"

"Please tell me you're not going to go there," he said, holding the knife by his side, "not here, not now, not ever."

"I'm sorry, but I had to ask. I need to know what I'm getting myself into."

"Getting into? C'mon Val, you know I take photos. Just take a gander at the walls around you," he voiced, waving the knife through the air.

"Yeah, but I didn't know they included women... young women," I paused, "half-naked women."

"Look," he said, still holding the knife. "What I do is my business. It doesn't concern you. If you think there's more going on, you're wrong, dead wrong."

"I'm sorry, but think of it from my perspective. What if you moved in with me and were home alone one day and some hot guy came knocking at my door asking for me, telling you that I have something of his. Wouldn't you wonder?"

"No."

"You wouldn't?" Crossing my arms, I glared at him. "Not even a little bit?"

"No, because it's none of my business." David's face reddened as his voice grew louder.

I figured I better drop it. I could never convince him to see my side, my point of view.

I retreated to the spare room, sat down at my desk, and stared out the window. I did some deep breathing as I tried to shake off the remnants of our first argument. In hindsight, it shouldn't have upset me as much as it did, but I allowed my emotions to get the best of me.

It brought me right back to our dinner that night at the harbor when I caught him leering at those two young women who had the same look as Kayla. I had the feeling he was attracted to those types of females and wondered what he was doing with me. I'm the complete opposite.

Flipping open my laptop, I clicked on a new document and gazed at the blank page. I tried forcing myself to write, but I couldn't concentrate. Ten minutes later, a knock sounded at the door.

David entered the room, placing a small bowl of salad in front of me.

"Thank you," I said, picking up the fork and piercing a chunk of avocado.

"Hey, I'm sorry about earlier."

"It's okay. I shouldn't have let it upset me."

"And I shouldn't have raised my voice at you, but I've been down that road so many times in the past. The bottom line is you have nothing to worry about."

"Okay."

Leaning against the wall by my desk, he chewed a mouthful of greens.

"I have a little surprise for you," he said.

"What's that?"

"To be honest, it's a surprise for both of us. I wasn't expecting it to happen so soon."

"Okay, now you're confusing me. What's going on?"

"Remember when I told you I'd like to live in Costa Rica someday."

"Yeah."

"Well, that someday has arrived."

"Wait, what? You're moving? When?"

"Next month," he said between bites.

"You can't be serious. I guess I'll have to move back to Vegas," I sighed.

"But that's not what you want to do. You were miserable there."

"Yeah, but I can't afford to stay here by myself. I just arrived and I don't even have a job. I only have a tiny bit of savings. I don't know anyone here."

"I was hoping you'd come with me?"

"To another country?"

"Why not?"

"But what are we going to do? Where are we going to live?"

"I have it all figured out. There's no need to worry."

"It seems a bit daunting to me," I rubbed the sides of my arms.

"How so?"

"First off, I don't know the language."

"There's nothing to be afraid of, I promise. And you can learn the language; it's easy. Besides, you'll be much safer there with me."

16

David

I almost lost her. We were up half the night discussing the pros and cons of moving to Costa Rica. It took some convincing on my part, but I couldn't answer all of her questions. I'm not a psychic; I can't predict the future. I can only prepare for the things I'm aware of and the knowledge I've gained.

When I mentioned to Val that she wouldn't have to work and could focus on writing her books, she became leery. What if they don't sell? What if I run out of money? What if something happens to me? What if something happens to you? So many 'what if's' that my head was spinning. I told her life holds no guarantees. She could take a chance or never know.

We finally came to an agreement when I offered her a backup plan. In the worst-case scenario, if it didn't work out, I would pay for her plane ticket home. She would have her car full of personal belongings waiting for her to start over again if need be.

After three hours of sleep, the first thing Val did was call Cindy for advice. Now, here we are, a week later, and Cindy's at the condo. She flew out for a few days to support her friend.

I sent them away earlier, treating them to a spa day—massages, facials, manicures, pedicures, the works. It will allow me to pack all of my essential items without them nosing around, asking a thousand questions. By the time they return to the condo, the goods will be locked up in suitcases, tucked safely away in my office, ready to go. I need to stay ahead of the game this time and not fall behind. One wrong move could cost a life.

When the gals returned home, all primped and pampered, I tell them to change clothes because I'm taking them out to dinner. I need to get to know Cindy a little better and see what she's all about. They say you can learn a great deal about someone by the friends they keep. I am interested in learning more about Val from Cindy's point of view.

Halfway through dinner, I am having trouble making the connection between the two. They are complete opposites. Cindy is boisterous and reminds me of one of my exes. She drinks like a fish and has downed three double martinis, flirting with everyone in sight, including me.

"David," Cindy says, reaching out, stroking a finger down my forearm, "you look so familiar."

I glance over and see Val fidgeting in her seat. She's clearly uncomfortable.

"I suppose I look like your average guy," I reply to her while looking at Val.

"Nope," she replies, her glass swaying, tiny drops of alcohol dotting the table. "I think I've seen you somewhere before."

"You've probably seen me at the hotel. I often stay there when I'm in Vegas. When I find something good, I tend to stick with it." Grinning, I turn my gaze to Val.

"I see tons of people in my job, many different faces." Cindy hiccups. "But you," she points, drawing a circle in the air, "you have one of those faces I wouldn't forget."

"Cindy, I think you need to lay off the martinis," Val pipes in.

"Whaaat? I'm having fun. I'm on vacation. Don't be such a party pooper."

"This isn't a party; it happens to be dinner." Val corrects her as if she's speaking to a child.

"You need to lighten up, Val. You're so uptight at

times." Picking up the cocktail stick, she slides the last olive into her mouth.

"Who's ready for dessert?" I clap, interrupting them before things intensify.

"I am," Cindy exclaims. "Something, umm, chocolatey," her eyes grow wide and her head swivels as she searches for the waiter. Spotting him, she starts snapping her fingers.

"What do you have that's chocolate?" she asks, her voice piercing the air as the waiter approaches the table.

"The molten chocolate lava cake is a favorite," he replies.

"Great, we'll all have it," she says, slurring her words.

"Correction," I intervene quickly to explain, "one cake and three spoons."

"Three spoons... ooh, we're gonna be like three's company." Cindy snorts, laughing out loud. "We're all gonna share with one another."

I glance over at Val, her face turning red as she mouths me an apology. Cindy is quite the handful. She definitely checks off all of the boxes of a wild and crazy party girl. But for me, three has never been company; it's always been a crowd.

"Cindy! Cut it out." Val gives her the evil eye. "You're shut off," she announces, pulling the martini away from her. "No more, you need to sober up."

"You're no fun. You're so vanilla," Cindy mocks while reaching for her drink. "Once again, it's good old vanilla Val to the rescue."

"Yeah, well, how many times have I saved your butt from bad situations?"

I gaze at Val and then at Cindy. Clearly, I have chosen the right one. Val is a good girl, the type who rescues her friends in times of need. She has her head on straight. She has morals.

"Too freaking many," Val hints when Cindy fails to reply.

"Where's your sense of adventure?" Cindy smirks, rolling her eyes.

The waiter returns with our dessert, and the ladies quiet down the second they dig into the cake, eating it like there's no tomorrow.

We arrive back at the condo, and Val helps a woozy Cindy to bed. It reminds me of my earlier days, of the hard partying nights when I'd stumble home from the local bar three sheets to the wind. My life was different back then; I didn't have a care in the world. I didn't know then what I know now. I hadn't a clue.

It would be easy to close my eyes and pretend all is well and nothing is wrong, but it's too late to turn back now. The seed has been planted, and I must complete the task.

Tonight's little episode confirms my choice. Val is the one. The light that shines within and surrounds her is precisely what I need. There's too much darkness in my life.

Val is the light, my shining light. She will be the one to protect me from the shadows.

Valerie

That night there was nothing but fog. Thick, heavy fog whirled in front of the dim headlights as we wound up the mountain. We couldn't see two feet ahead of us.

As the old pickup truck chugged along the road, the springs of the worn leather seats squeaked with each turn. I reached out for David's hand, lacing my fingers through his as he squeezed them, comforting me while sensing my fear.

When we arrived in Costa Rica, David had arranged for his friend to pick us up at the airport. Slim, a tall, lanky man was waiting for us under an exit sign. Dressed in a checkered shirt and dirty wranglers, he tipped his cowboy hat from his ponytailed white hair and greeted me. David introduced us, telling me Slim was a local farmer-turned-friend who owned a pineapple farm two hours from town. He also ran a nearby ecolodge and had offered David one of the casitas for us to stay at.

When I shook Slim's hand, he had an odd look on his face. He seemed taken aback to see David with someone. I sensed he might have expected David to be alone. I wondered if David forgot to tell him I would be accompanying him or moving with him to Costa Rica.

It took less than a month for David and me to pack up the condo and ship his belongings. Our relationship moved at a lightning-fast speed with no time for second thoughts. It was challenging to keep up with him at times. I had no idea where he got all of his energy from. He was always on the go—always out and about, keeping busy with work and friends.

Even though I was alone most of the time at the condo, I didn't get much writing done. Whatever items we didn't sell or giveaway, he put me in charge of packing and coordinating shipment. I ended up packing most of my things in my Jeep, and Cindy drove it back to Vegas. She thought my belongings would be safer with her, at the house, in the event I ever needed to return to the states.

David kept saying I wouldn't want to return once we arrived in Central America and established our life together. He said there were important things he needed to share but could only tell me once we arrived in Costa Rica. He looked deep into my eyes and asked me to trust him completely. He promised me he had my best interest at heart. Because of the strong bond, that is, the special connection I felt with him, I decided to trust him. I had fallen in love.

"How much farther do we have to go?" I asked. Taking deep breaths, I tried soothing the uneasiness in my stomach.

"We're almost there," David replied, staring out the window.

David and Slim made small talk during the ride, discussing local farms and different kinds of fruits and plants Slim wanted to grow. David seemed genuinely interested and talked about starting his own mini-farm.

Two hours later, we had finally reached our destination. As the truck climbed a long dirt driveway, it came to a stop in front of a row of casitas with colorful lights shining from them.

When I exited the truck, the first thing I noticed was the remoteness of the area. Tall, dense trees with huge, oversized leaves covered the property, concealing it from any houses nearby. From what I could see, it didn't appear like the manicured gardens of the bed-and-breakfast we had occupied months before—a stark contrast. We were deep in the overgrown jungle in the middle of nowhere. The only familiar sound was the continuous buzzing of the night insects.

Slim unlocked the door to one of the casitas and stepped inside, placing the key on a small tree stump table. I followed David, noticing the tiny living area with two rattan chairs.

"I filled the fridge with the basics to cover you for a few days," Slim said. "Ring me if you need anything."

"Thank you, my friend. I appreciate the hospitality." David smiled, patting him on the shoulder.

Slim leaned in close to David, whispering something under his breath. The only words I could make out were 'ex-wife,' 'no,' and 'angel.' Slim then glanced over in my direction and shot me a half smile. He waved goodbye and swiftly turned on his heel, closing the door behind him.

Gazing out the window, I watched the headlights of his truck slowly fade into the darkness. At that moment, a sense of foreboding washed over me as an eerie presence surrounded me.

What was I thinking of—moving to a strange country with a near stranger?

David sneaked up from behind, wrapping his arms around my waist. My body stiffened.

"You seem lost in thought. Is everything okay?"

"Yeah," I replied hesitantly. "I just felt a weird sensation."

"It's been a long day; maybe you're just tired."

"Maybe."

"You're all tensed up," he said, his hands sliding up my back as he began massaging my shoulders.

I wasn't in the mood to be touched. I wanted to be left alone. I needed some time to sort out my sudden feeling of déjà-vu.

"What did Slim say to you?"

"Why do you ask?" His hands stopped moving and remained still. They felt heavy at the base of my neck.

"I thought I heard him say something about a wife."

"If you must know, he said you look like my ex-wife." He took a step back, releasing his grip.

"Which one?" I asked, immediately thinking I shouldn't have.

"It doesn't matter," he snapped. Walking away, he went into the kitchen area.

"So, he's met your wife before?" There was a momentary pause.

"He saw a photo of her a long time ago."

I stood at the window, collecting my thoughts. I heard a cabinet open and the clanging of a spoon against a cup.

"You're right; it's been a long day. I need to change out of these clothes and get some sleep." I turned and reached for my luggage.

"The bedroom is around the corner behind that half wall. I'm going to make some tea. I'll be in shortly," he replied.

I entered the tiny bedroom, quickly changed into my pajamas and walked back into the kitchen. I wanted to apologize to David for asking too many questions and upsetting him. I didn't want us to go to bed angry.

He was leaning against the small counter, sipping his tea, staring off in the distance. I went over to him.

"Want some?" he offered, holding the cup out to me.

Reaching for it, I took a sip and then tried to give it back to him.

"Drink some more; it'll help you sleep," he pushed the cup toward me.

I took a few more sips. It didn't taste like much and was kind of weak.

"Okay," he said, taking the cup from me. "I'm going to clean up. I'll be in shortly."

I smiled, feeling a bit better that we ended the night on a happier note.

After washing my face and brushing my teeth, I crawled into bed. As I waited for David to join me, I felt it again, that strange sensation. I had hoped by the time morning came, my anxiety would have disappeared.

The next morning I woke up to a glass of orange juice by the bedside. Rubbing my eyes, I sat up to take a sip and soon heard David mumbling in the background. I arose from bed and with glass in hand padded into the living area and over to the kitchenette.

Dressed in his boxers, David was scrambling eggs and had his cell phone in the crook of his neck. When he turned around, he saw me standing there.

"Okay, my friend," he spoke into the phone, "we'll be ready." Pressing a button, he set the phone on the counter and smiled at me.

"Good morning, sunshine, did you sleep well?"

"I tossed and turned for a while, trying to get comfortable, and then I had a very frightening dream."

"Oh yeah, what was it about?"

"I don't remember all of it, but I was trapped in a shack in the middle of nowhere. I kept screaming, but no one could hear me."

He didn't say a word as he grabbed two dishes from the wooden shelf above him.

I wasn't sure if I should tell him the worst part of my dream—about the body lying on the ground near the shack —a woman's dead body.

"Thanks for the juice," I said, raising my glass in the air.

"Nothing better than fresh squeezed to start your day." Spooning a handful of eggs on a plate, he slid it in front of me.

"Toast will be up in a minute, and Slim will be here in an hour to pick us up." He turned to the small pot of coffee and poured himself a cup. "He's letting me borrow his truck for the day. We'll need to make a quick stop and drop him off at his farm."

"Okay." I took a bite of the eggs. They were loaded with cheese.

"So, I have a little surprise for you."

"Another one? So soon? You're a man full of surprises." I forced a smile.

David held my gaze, staring at me over the rim of his cup. His dark eyes suddenly appeared darker, penetrating through me and sending a chill up my spine.

18

David

The look on her face when we pull up to the house is priceless. I remain silent while she takes in the surroundings, anticipating her thoughts. When we exit the vehicle, we walk side by side along the long gravel pathway.

It's a beautiful day; the sun shines bright in the mid-morning sky. A handful of large puffy clouds off in the distance hint at a possible rain shower later this afternoon. In the jungle, the weather changes throughout the day. The various microclimates are one of the reasons I chose this place. I like variety. As they say, variety is the spice of life.

"Who lives here?" she asks, as we draw closer to the

wrought iron gate that separates us from a second walkway.

"We do," I reply boastfully.

"What?" Her eyes widen and her mouth drops open. "You can't be serious."

Unlocking the gate, we continue along the stone paved trail leading up to the front door.

"This place looks abandoned," she comments.

"No," shaking my head, I chuckle to myself. "It just needs a little more work. It's not quite finished yet."

"How come you didn't tell me about it?"

"I told you I had planned on moving here one day."

"Yeah, I know… but this house… you never mentioned you already had a house here."

"I wanted it to be a surprise." Slipping the keys from my pocket, I first unlock the steel security door and then proceed to open the hand-carved wood door. From the corner of my eye, I see Val gazing up at the windows.

"What's with all the bars?" she asks. "It looks like a jail cell."

"Everyone down here has bars on their windows for protection."

"So much for safety," she sucks her teeth. "You told me I'd be safe here with you."

"And you will. I'll make sure of it. We'll be much safer here than we were in LA."

As I step inside, Val follows close behind, creeping her way into the main living area. She stops in the middle of the room and stands there gazing all around.

"It looks much bigger from the outside," she says, her voice bouncing off the concrete wall.

"I don't need a lot of space." Walking away, I step over the threshold. "Come over here and check out the master suite."

Poking her head inside, she glances at the spartan furnishings. A mattress sits atop a teak wood frame, and a matching teak armoire stands against the wall.

"It's a tiny bedroom but at least it's half furnished."

"Correction, fully furnished. Less is more in my book."

Turning around, she steps into the bathroom.

"I'm guessing blue is your favorite color," she remarks, running her fingers over the tiled countertop.

"The secret is out." I smile.

"It's a lot of blue for one room. I personally would have broken up the color scheme, maybe a more neutral color along the walls."

"I'll admit that I don't have the best eye when it comes to interior design. Building things is my forte. I'm hoping you can help me decorate the place."

"Sure," she murmurs as she walks back to the main room. "I guess it does have potential."

Making my way over to the side and rear walls, I pull back the striped curtains to expose five sliding glass doors, or as I like to call them, my floor-to-ceiling windows.

"Now, for the best part of the house, the magnificent view."

"View? Of what, the trees?" A trace of confusion

crosses her face. "There's nothing but trees."

"Wait until you see my neighbors," I motion for her to come closer.

She ambles toward me and stands gazing out the middle door.

"Neighbors? There's not another house in sight." Peering through the glass, she squints and turns her head. She looks to the left and then to the right.

Unlocking one of the doors, we step out onto an expansive wood deck.

"Hold my hand," I say, reaching out for hers. "I still need to install railings out here."

Two minutes later, the screeching begins. A bright green parrot flies by, flits through the trees and lands on one of the branches. Behind the bird, brilliant blue butterflies flutter in the air, dancing in the gentle breeze.

"Wow!" Her eyes light up. "They're so beautiful, so colorful."

"It's like this every day... parrots, toucans, blue morphos... sometimes a capuchin monkey or two will swing by to say hello."

"Really?"

"Yeah, but you'll need to remember not to leave your shoes out on the deck. The monkeys sometimes take things that don't belong to them."

"Cute," she shrieks, letting out a tiny giggle. "Burglar monkeys."

"I would imagine the animals could inspire your writing,

help you create stories."

"Yeah, there are so many cool creatures here; I could have a whole jungle book series."

"Maybe your first book could be about a monkey who swings from the trees wearing sneakers."

She gazes over at me shaking her head. "Seriously?"

"Why not? Isn't that the beauty of writing? You can create any story you want."

She walks up to me and stares into my eyes. "So what's your story? Why do I get the feeling you're hiding something?" Two questions that drop out of nowhere.

"What would I be hiding?" I'm not prepared for an interrogation.

"I don't know. I guess because we're still getting to know each other. I guess because you never told me you already had a house here." She pauses to take a breath. "Things are happening a little too fast for me."

"So, I take it you're having second thoughts?"

"I don't know. Everything's new, and there are so many things that are unknown."

"But I thought you were an adventurous type of gal. Did I get it wrong?"

"You're the one who likes action-adventures."

"And you're the one who likes mysteries."

"Thrillers," she adds. "I also like old-fashioned psychological thrillers."

"Well, then, think of our new life together as an action-adventure with a tinge of thriller."

19

Valerie

A few weeks later, the house was looking more like home. We purchased a gray futon and a dining set, and David let me pick out some new curtains for the glass doors. But the most important part, at least for me, was finally having the internet hooked up.

I had been out of touch with the world, only having access to snippets of local news when we were out and about running errands. Most of the TVs at the bars and restaurants were tuned into either sports or news channels. Everything was spoken in Spanish and I had no idea what they were saying. But David did his best to translate for me although he didn't speak the language a hundred percent.

When I turned on the computer, there were a bunch of emails from Cindy. As I opened the messages, each one more dire than the other, I sensed her concern.

Hey, Val, wanted to touch base. Please call or email when you can.

Are you okay?

Why aren't you returning my messages?

I tried texting and calling your phone, but it goes directly to voicemail.

Val, where the hell are you?

Pick up your damn phone, Val!

If I don't hear from you in the next forty-eight hours, I'm coming down to find you.

My heart sank as I quickly sent her a reply. I had been so busy with the house and all that I felt bad for not reaching out to her sooner. I went into the bedroom and grabbed my phone to check for texts. When I pressed the lower button, the screen didn't light up. For a minute I thought the battery was dead because I hadn't used it in a while. After toying with the buttons, I soon realized it had been turned off, but I didn't remember turning it off.

David had a local cell phone and since I was always with him when we were out, I didn't need to keep mine on me at all times. He had promised to buy me a second phone with a local number so I wouldn't rack up hundreds of dollars in phone bills, but he never got around to it.

Sliding the phone into my pocket, I went back to the kitchen for a bottle of water. Within minutes it was ringing.

"Hello?"

"Damn, Val. Where the hell have you been?" Cindy shrilled.

"I take it you got my email."

"Yes, finally, I've been waiting forever to hear from you."

"I said I was sorry. You have no idea what it's been like the past few weeks. Things aren't as easy down here; it's a lot harder to get things done. It took weeks to get internet service."

"And phone service, too, huh?"

"No, for some reason, my phone was shut off. I hadn't been checking it because I—"

"I was worried sick about you."

"I know. I already said I was sorry."

"Well, I'm glad you're alive. Listen, there's something I need to tell you."

"What? What is it? Is everything okay there?"

"Yeah, everything's fine. Nicole has been getting on my nerves and work has been crazy, but I'm dealing with it."

"So, what's going on?"

"It's about David."

"What about him?"

"Do you know he has a dating profile?"

"What dating profile?"

"So you don't."

"No, but how do you know?"

"Because he came up on my reverse match."

"Reverse match? What are you talking about?"

"My profile alerts me when people search for someone like me."

"Someone like you? Why would he be searching for someone like you?"

A moment of silence hung between us. Cindy let out a long, huffed breath.

"I guess his search preferences matched mine. Gosh, Val, I don't know all the details."

"I'm sorry I didn't mean that. My words came out wrong. I just don't understand. I'm confused."

"That's why I'm calling you. I wanted you to be aware of it."

"I don't know what to think right now."

"Well, on the bright side, I don't think he has logged in lately. So maybe he posted it before he met you."

"Can you send me a link? I need to see it for myself."

"Look, Val, I don't want to upset you. Maybe you should ask David about it."

"What the heck? How do I casually bring up a dating profile? He'll think I've been snooping."

"Okay, okay, I'll send it. But don't tell him I told you. I don't want to be in the middle of this."

"I won't."

"Promise?"

"I promise."

"And keep your damn phone on in case I need to reach you."

"I will. Talk to you soon."

I ended the call, my hands trembling as I slid the phone back into my pocket. My heart raced and my stomach churned at the thought of David's dating profile.

I reached for the water bottle, took a quick sip, and walked over to the glass doors. Sliding one open, I stepped out onto the deck. I stood there for a while, inhaling the fresh air and trying to calm my nerves.

Despite the sounds of the birds chirping and the wind rustling through the trees, I couldn't relax. Visions of Kayla crept through my mind, followed by the two young women at the harbor restaurant in LA. They all shared something in common. They were tall, skinny blondes—just like Cindy.

My thoughts then drifted to David's ex-wives as I began wondering what they looked like. I knew it shouldn't matter, but I couldn't help feeling a bit unnerved and somewhat betrayed.

My phone chimed. Pulling it out, I held it by my side, hesitant to look at the message. I wasn't sure I wanted to see it because once I saw it; I wouldn't be able to unsee it.

Taking a deep breath, I tapped on the screen. Cindy's email appeared, and I opened the link. There he was, the man of my dreams, on a dating site.

I stared at the photo and then at his profile name, 'Now You Behave.' *How fitting*, I thought. His tagline read, 'Fit, fun, gentleman seeks adventurous woman to travel the world.'

Stuffing the phone back in my pocket, I didn't know

whether to laugh or cry but knew I didn't have the time or energy to deal with it. At that moment, the sound of a rumbling engine grew near.

I gazed out through the trees and saw a blue pickup truck making its way down the main road toward the house. David had taken the bus earlier to run a few errands in town, so I figured it was someone giving him a ride back.

It was the first time he had left me alone at the house and I was uneasy. No matter how many times I told him how frightened I felt, he ignored me. Oblivious to my feelings, he had a hard time understanding my point of view. Not only was he much more familiar with the area but he also had no problem adapting as he thrived on new experiences.

My senses went into overdrive. It had taken me a while to adjust to the house and my new surroundings. Every sound was new and each snapping of a branch had me thinking someone was outside casing the place. Most of the men carried machetes and my mind often wandered to the worst-case scenario.

There was an ongoing saying about Americans living there. It went something like this: 'It's not *if* your house will get broken into; it's a matter of *when*.'

Day and night, I prayed for our safety. I had mentioned to David about maybe getting a dog for protection who could also be my companion. Each time we went into town, I would see starving mangy mutts, wanting to take them all home. It broke my heart to see so many strays roaming around the area.

I soon heard a voice and then footsteps coming up the walkway along with the jingling of metal. As I walked back inside the house, I went to the front door to unlock it. Trailing behind David was a big black dog with icy blue eyes. With his tail wagging and his tongue lolling out of his mouth, he made his way toward me.

"Say hello to Max," David said, a smile forming on his face.

"Hi, Max! Aren't you a handsome boy?" I reached down to pet him and he jumped up, licking my face.

"He's friendly too," he winked.

"Who does he belong to?"

"Us."

"Really?" I replied, my eyes widening.

"Yeah, he was hanging out in the yard of the guy I bought the truck from."

I gazed over his shoulder at the beaten-up truck parked in the driveway. "That old thing?" I pointed. "That jalopy is yours?"

"Ours," he replied proudly. "Now, we don't have to borrow Slim's truck or take the bus when we want to go to town."

I stood there, shaking my head. "Is it reliable? It doesn't look as though it would go very far."

"Don't worry. I'm going to have a mechanic check it

over this week. Besides, Max didn't have a problem with it. He loved hanging out in the back and going for a ride."

"I better not see him riding in the back of that thing; it's way too dangerous," I fumed. "He could fall out."

"But everyone does it down here. I've even seen them transport horses in the backs of their trucks."

"Please don't tell me these things." I cried out, putting my hands over my ears. "How can people be so careless?"

I glanced down to see Max sitting there, panting heavily, and staring up at me. "I promise you, boy, I will always protect you," I said softly, patting his head.

20

David

I retrieve the groceries and the large bag of dog food from the truck. As I make my way along the walkway back toward the house, I sense something's off with Val. I thought she would have been more excited about the dog since all she ever talks about is safety. I expected a different reaction.

I have another surprise in store for her but decide to save it for later. I am slowly learning that Val doesn't like too much information thrown at her all at once. I have the feeling she is overwhelmed with the move and I'm hoping she isn't having second thoughts. I don't know what I'll do if she leaves me. I will do everything in my power to make sure she stays.

I have to act fast and put things in order, so she won't have any reason to leave. I want to make things easy on her, so she can have time to focus on her writing.

"Here, let me help you," she says, reaching out to carry a bag of groceries.

Max circles around us, whining and sniffing each bag, anxiously waiting for his food. Val finds one of the plastic bowls I bought and fills it with kibble. When she places it on the floor, Max starts crunching away. She unpacks the remaining items, lining them up on the counter.

"Peach wine?" she questions. Holding the bottle up in front of her, she examines the label. "I've never seen this kind before."

"Yeah, there are all sorts of cool products here. It makes shopping very interesting." I watch as she stares at the bottle, a blank expression frozen on her face as if she's trying to avoid me.

"You can open it if you want," I suggest.

A half crooked smile forms on her lips as she places the wine on the counter.

"Okay, what's going on? Did something happen while I was away?"

Hesitating, she gently strokes the top of Max's head as he sits next to her panting.

"I talked to Cindy today," she replies, lowering her gaze.

"Oh, really? What did she have to say?"

"She was worried about me because she hadn't been able to reach me."

"You still have your phone, right?"

"Yeah, but it was turned off."

"Why did you shut it off?"

"I didn't. That's the strange part. If I did, I don't remember."

"Listen, we've had a lot going on. You've been busy since we arrived. Maybe things have been a bit overwhelming for you."

"Yeah, it's going to take some time getting used to being here. Everything is so different."

I watch as she struggles to open the bottle.

"Here, let me open it for you." Gripping the bottle, I twist the cap off while she reaches into the cabinet for wine glasses.

"Twist off," she remarks, raising an eyebrow.

After filling both glasses halfway, we retreat to the living area. Val takes a seat on the futon, crossing her legs underneath her and slowly sips her wine. She avoids looking at me and focuses her attention on Max, who lays peacefully beside her on the floor. I see he's made himself right at home.

But back to Val. I sense something is bothering her. She appears melancholy and on the verge of tears. I hate when women cry. I need to avert her sadness.

"So I was thinking. Maybe you'd like some help around the house."

"Help?" she scoffs, her eyebrows scrunching together.

"You need to understand something. It's customary to hire a local woman to help the lady of the house."

"With what?"

"With the basics, you know, cooking and cleaning."

"But this place is so tiny," she says, waving her hand above her. "It's barely big enough for the two of us," she gazes at Max, "er, three of us."

"Then maybe we have her come a few days a week to start."

"Does that mean we'll have to interview someone?"

"Actually, I already have someone in mind."

"Oh, who?"

"Her name is Conchita. She's a friend of Slim's housekeeper and she's in need of work."

"Hmm, I guess if you think we need help."

"My belongings are due to arrive tomorrow from LA. Conchita can help you unpack the boxes, sort things and put them away. Maybe she can also teach you some local recipes, you know, things like that."

"Okay, whatever you say."

That's right, whatever I say.

While swirling my wine, I gaze at the sliding door and see spots of water dotting the glass. There's a rumbling, a cracking of thunder and then a sharp bolt of lightning flashes in the sky. Within moments the water droplets turn into streaks as the rain pelts down.

I glance over at Val, a look of unease spreading across her face as she stares out into the darkness.

"You okay over there."

"This place is kind of spooky at night. You can't see out."

"You're right, you can't. But if someone were outside, they could see in."

"They could? If someone were outside right now, they could see us?"

"Yeah, they could see into the house. Someone could be watching us," I wiggle my brows.

"That's a frightful thought." She quivers.

"Think of it this way. In the daytime, when you are inside, you can see out. But when the sun is shining, with the reflection of light, if someone was outside, they'd have a hard time seeing in."

"So at night, it's reversed?"

"Yes."

"Why?"

"Because at night, when it's dark and there's a light on inside, you can see in, but you can't see out."

Valerie

I had just stepped out of the shower and was drying off when Max started growling and barking. In between his loud woofs, I heard a soft knocking at the front door.

"David, can you get that?" I called out.

There was no reply.

Wondering where he was, I quickly threw on a T-shirt and shorts and rushed into the kitchen. When I opened the door, a petite woman in a red dress with a long braid of black hair stood before me. A look of terror filled her eyes as they widened at the sight of Max. I immediately grasped Max's collar, holding it tight, but he lunged toward her, pulling my arm and throwing me off balance.

"Tengo miedo a los perros," she screamed as she bolted from the house. I had no idea what she was saying but figured it had something to do with Max.

I stood in the doorway and watched the woman run toward David as he came strolling up the driveway, his machete swinging by his side. After tucking the machete into its leather sheath attached to his belt, he reached out his arms to give her a hug. Still holding onto Max's collar, we jogged to the side of the house where I secured him on the dog run.

Speaking of being terrified, those darn machetes scare me to death. It seemed everyone in town had them and each time I saw one, horrible pictures filled my mind. I imagined a deranged killer roaming the jungle, slicing and chopping up people.

David would laugh and call me crazy, telling me I had an overactive imagination. He assured me people only used them as tools—to prepare fruit and clear the thick underbrush that grew wildly everywhere. Some of the plants and tree leaves were so huge you could hide a child behind them, or a small woman who was now back at our doorstep.

David had his arm draped around her trembling shoulder to comfort her. "Val, I'd like you to meet Conchita."

"Hola," she spoke softly, afraid to look at me.

"Nice to meet you." Smiling, I reached out to shake her hand. "Please come in."

"¿Dónde está el perro?" she asked, her head swiveling left and right.

"She's asking where the dog is," David translated for me.

"Oh, I tied him to his run," I pointed. "The coast is clear."

"Está atado ahora," David explained, winking at her. "I told her he's tied up now."

I admit that not knowing the language was challenging. Despite practicing an hour a day, I was having a difficult time getting up to speed. If David were to talk to her about me, I wouldn't have a clue about what they were saying.

"Why don't you make us some coffee?" David asked as he pulled out a chair for Conchita.

"¿Quieres un café?" he turned to her.

"No, no," she mumbled, reaching inside her pocket. "Té, por favor."

She placed a small cotton sack on the table pointing to it. "Una taza de agua caliente."

"Of course, a cup of hot water," he nodded. "Val, please boil some water. We're having tea instead." He leaned in closer to her and they began talking under their breath and sharing laughs. I guessed there was something funny about the tea.

As I stood at the sink filling the kettle, I could feel her stare boring into me. I wondered what she thought of me, the Americana who didn't speak a shred of Spanish. Dreading the thought of David having to translate for me continuously, I promised myself I'd study more.

After placing the kettle on the stove, I took a seat at the

table next to David. He reached for the cotton sack, untied it, and took a long whiff. He then pulled out three teabags that appeared to be homemade. They had colorful strings stapled to them with tiny handwritten tags at the end.

"¿Que tipo?" he questioned while holding one. "What kind?"

"Tranquilo," Conchita softly replied, pointing to the tag.

"Ahh, like chamomile tea to calm the nerves, relieve stress."

"Sí, sí." She smiled.

"Hey Val, you could use a few of these." He chuckled, waving the bag in the air.

"Very funny," I quipped.

I rose from my chair to retrieve the kettle and teacups, returning to the table with them. The moment I set a cup in front of Conchita, she dropped a teabag into the steaming water.

David casually conversed with her while stirring and sipping his tea between sentences. I sat back and listened, testing myself while trying to understand a word here and there. Off in the distance, I heard the low hum of an engine as it drew near. Soon after, Max began barking.

I stood up and walked over to the glass door. Slim's truck, covered in mud and loaded with boxes, made its way up the driveway toward the house. A horn honked and David jumped up from the table. Conchita got up seconds later and followed him out the door.

I quickly pulled on my rain boots and went outside to

help them unload the truck. Everyone wore rubber boots as you were either walking in the rain or trudging through the wet, muddy grounds of the jungle.

When we were out running errands one day, I had eyed a pair of leopard print rain boots. All I did was comment on them and David bought them for me the next day. He was generous like that. I didn't want for anything; he was very thoughtful, always surprising me with little gifts. He said it was a Costa Rican tradition that the men would bring small trinkets home to their women. Yesterday it was a colorful, beaded bracelet.

One by one, we carried the boxes inside the house, stacking them against the wall in the living room. Four sets of muddy footprints trailed across the floor and as I reached for the mop, Conchita caught me sighing.

"Mañana, mañana. Te ayudaré a limpiar." She reached out toward me.

I guessed she said something about tomorrow and helping me with something. I pulled out my phone and asked her to tell me again as I tried translating the words. I was close. She said she wanted to help me clean tomorrow.

"Sí, gracias," I replied, proud to say, 'yes, thanks' on my own.

Nodding her head, she smiled at me and I hoped it was the beginning of a new friendship.

Fifteen boxes and ten suitcases later, we said our goodbyes. Slim had offered to give Conchita a ride home. I brought Max back inside, fed him his dinner, and then flopped down on the futon, exhausted from the day's activities. I must've drifted off because I woke to find David tapping me on the shoulder.

"Hey, you okay? You zonked out on me."

"I don't know why I'm so tired," I sat up, yawning and rubbing at my eyes.

"Perhaps the Tranquilo tea worked its magic on you," he said while drawing the curtains.

"I guess. I feel like I hit a wall. Think I'm going to call it a night."

"Okay, get some rest. I'll be in shortly. I'm going to check my email."

As I padded my way into the bedroom with Max trailing behind me, an uneasy feeling washed over me. Through my fog of fatigue, David's dating profile popped up into my head. I tried hard to push it away. When I slipped into bed, hugging my pillow, Max jumped up and cuddled beside me.

Tears soon filled my eyes as I lay there, gently stroking his fur. I couldn't help wonder if Mr. fit & fun was looking for a new travel partner.

22

DAVID

I wonder if Val sensed it wasn't the first time I had met Conchita. I mean, the woman ran straight into my arms while she watched from the doorway. Val's a sharp cookie and nothing gets passed her. I must say it's a good trait to have here in the jungle. One should always be alert for hidden dangers.

Once again, I detected fear in her eyes when she saw me with my machete. Who knows what kinds of scenarios she conjures up in that writer's mind of hers? I'm concerned, though, that she sometimes confuses fiction with reality.

In all my years down here, there had been only one incident and it was totally avoidable. At least that's what I tell myself; it's how I cope with it.

I'm not sure if Val would ever be ready for me to share that story. To be honest, I'm not sure I even want to relive that night. For now, it'll stay buried in my mind. I'll have to be more observant this time and mustn't let frivolous distractions get in the way.

I log into my email and scroll down the page. Now there's something I haven't seen in a while. I haven't visited that site in months. I click on the message to read what it says.

CutieC has winked at you. Log in now to view her profile. CutieC could be your perfect match.

I hesitate for a moment with Val in the next room. Gazing over my shoulder, I check to make sure the bedroom door is closed. I decide to log into my account to window shop only. You know the saying, 'you can look, but you can't touch.' All men like to look and all women need to get over it.

I stare at the screen and narrow my eyes. I'm mystified. I know that gal, know her face. It can't be her, can it?

CutieC. Such an interesting moniker for a scantily clad, skinny blonde.

I stare at her profile picture as she stares back, studying her two-sizes-too-small, low cut red dress. She's slightly bent over and blowing a kiss at me.

I lean back in my chair, crossing my arms over my chest and study the photo for a few more minutes. I wonder if she knows it's me.

I click back to my profile picture. There I am coming out of a swimming pool gripping the handrails. My hair's slicked back, and I'm wearing dark sunglasses. Granted, the photo is ten years old when I was twenty pounds lighter.

Maybe she didn't recognize me. Still, I ponder as I glance through her photo album.

CutieC is the typical Vegas girl. Every photo is ridiculously posed and airbrushed to the hilt. Dancing atop the bar in another skimpy outfit with a cocktail spilling from her hand. Eating sushi with chopsticks in an exaggerated manner while seated at a table with a gaggle of giggling girlfriends. Sitting at a slot machine in a jam-packed casino, sticking her tongue out while pulling the lever.

I stop and linger on the last photo. A sly smile forms on my lips. There they are the two of them at work dressed in their uniforms. They're leaning into each other with their arms out from their sides holding their drink-filled trays. Their eyes shine while pursing their lips for the person taking their photo.

A pang of jealousy pings my gut. Who is my girl making kissy faces at? Who is the person behind the camera? A coworker? An ex-boyfriend?

A whining and scratching sound jostles me from my thoughts. I rise from the table and softly stride over to the bedroom door. I slowly open it, careful not to wake Val as Max bolts from the room. He circles my legs twice and then runs over to the front door.

Val must've forgotten to let him out before bedtime. Opening the door, I flick on the floodlights as he trots outside, disappearing into the night.

I don't know why she insists on keeping him in the house. He's a watchdog; he belongs outside guarding the house. I don't want that smelly mutt in our bed. Scratch that, my bed. I paid for it.

I call the shots around here. I make the rules. But Val sometimes seems to forget. She needs to be reminded of the pecking order. She will need to become more submissive if she's going to be with a man like me. She will need to learn her place in the world—my world.

I log out of the website and close the laptop. Shuffling over to the front door, I open it and give a low whistle, calling Max back inside. From the corner of my eye, I see something move between the trees. A blurred figure passes through the ray of light.

"Max, is that you," I say, trying to keep my voice down.

Slipping my feet into my jungle Mocs, I close the door behind me and head down the walkway. The clopping of my shoes hitting the ground mixes with the chirping of crickets and the low hum of insects.

"Max, where are you?" I call out again a bit louder this time.

I stop and do a three-sixty, scanning the back yard. There is no sign of him. He must be off on an adventure and will come home when he tires of hunting.

As I trod along the path, I catch a glimpse of a dark shape appearing and disappearing in a flash.

I tell myself it's not real that I'm seeing things. Perhaps there's a stray tree branch dangling in front of the floodlights causing a shadow. Surely, if someone was out here, Max would've picked up on the scent.

I call out for Max one last time and then make my way back toward the house. When I arrive at the door, I glance up at the two floodlights. No tree limbs are hanging near them. Nothing is blocking them. The only thing near the lights is the security camera, which I still need to hook up. I need to stay on top of things this time around—no more mistakes.

Off in the distance, the grunting of howler monkeys echoes through the air, their sounds sending chills up my spine. My ex was terrified of them. The first time she heard them roar, she nearly jumped out of her skin. She said the sounds of the jungle would haunt her dreams.

I pause for a moment, wondering if she's here, wondering if she's haunting me while I'm awake.

23

Valerie

I was angry to find Max outside when I woke up the next morning. He was crying at the front door, visibly shaken and covered in mud. Once again, David was nowhere to be found. He didn't leave me a note; there was no message waiting for me. With each passing day, he seemed to become more distant.

After feeding Max and giving him a quick bath, I made myself some extra strong coffee. I hoped to combat the awful headache that was pounding in my skull. The tea from the night before had given me a horrible stomach ache soon after I drank it. And then the dream I had. One word describes it, bizarre. I could only imagine what was in Conchita's home-brewed potion.

With my mug in hand, I headed outside to the deck, Max at my heels, trailing behind me. The jungle was alive with a symphony of sounds, the scent of fresh rain filling the air. A variety of birdsong and distant humming entwined with the lush foliage and giant ferns. Towering trees with their moss-covered trunks and limbs reached high into the sky. At that moment, everything felt magical.

Taking a sip of coffee, I admired the great beauty and peacefulness that surround me. Max barked at two green parrots that flew by and landed on a branch in front of me. With their heads twitching, they began chattering and studying me. I wondered what they were talking about and curious if they understood Spanish.

Most days, David would set a variety of fruit on the deck for them. They usually came by each morning to eat breakfast. I didn't see any remnants of banana peels or half-eaten papaya, so he must've forgotten their breakfast.

As the parrots took flight, Max went running after them. After five full gallops, he stopped in his tracks dangerously close to the edge of the deck. Crouched down, he remained there, panting and peering below. I quickly grabbed hold of his collar and guided him down to the yard to his run. As much as I hated tying him up, he seemed safer when secured.

When I returned to the kitchen for a second cup of coffee, Max began barking again. Peeking out the window over the sink, I saw Conchita standing there in a bright orange dress holding a small bag. I unlocked and opened the door.

"Good morning," I said, stepping aside to let her into the house.

"Buenos días," she spoke softly.

"Please come in," I motioned.

"Gracias," she nodded her head. Holding her bag tightly, she stepped over the threshold.

"¿Café?" I asked, pointing to the coffee pot on the counter.

"No, no. Té."

Once again, she pulled out a small cotton sack full of teabags, placing it on the table. How could I forget the woman who only drinks tea? I boiled some water and then refilled my cup with the last of the coffee. I wasn't going anywhere near her suspicious sachets. It took a whole pot of coffee to vanquish my headache.

"¿David está aquí?" Glancing around, she appeared to be looking for David.

"David isn't here," I replied, pausing for a moment. I pointed to the floor, shaking my head, "No in casa."

She gave me an odd look.

"I don't know where he went... no dónde." Throwing my hands in the air, I shrugged my shoulders, hoping she would understand what I meant by the gesture.

As we sat drinking our beverages, she gazed up at me every few seconds and gave me a half smile. She seemed nervous around me, but I couldn't figure out why. I was trying my best to converse with her and thought I gave off a friendly vibe.

For fifteen minutes, we sat in uncomfortable silence until David came waltzing through the door. Conchita immediately jumped up to greet him as a faithful dog does for his master. I waited to see if maybe she was also going to lick his face.

I watched as he enveloped her in another welcoming hug. David was a hugger and hugged everyone he met. I assumed he did it to make her feel comfortable and put her at ease. They exchanged a handful of animated words for a minute. I deciphered three of them.

David walked over to the table and bent down, giving me a half hug and a tiny peck on the cheek. "Conchita said she's here to help you unpack the boxes."

"Okay," slightly pulling away, my eyes darting between them. "Where have you been all morning?"

"Slim needed my help with something and then I stopped at the nursery on the way back. I picked up some new plants and flowers for the garden. Wait until you see them." Smiling, he filled his water bottle and headed back out the door.

Conchita and I spent the next few hours unpacking most of the boxes and putting things away. One box remained closed and I set it next to the futon in the corner. Conchita had accidentally opened it and started pulling out David's folders full of paperwork. She may not have understood the word 'private' scribbled on it in blue ink.

When I put the files back in the box, I couldn't help notice one of the folders labeled 'insurance.' It caught my eye because it had my name written on the front of it. Conchita watched closely as I paused briefly, studying it. At that moment, I had offered to make us lunch but she quickly stood up, mumbling something about an autobús and casa.

She gathered her bag, waved at me, and then showed herself out the door. I went over to the sink to rinse out the cups and gazed out the kitchen window. David was kneeling on the ground with an array of flowering plants by his side. Conchita walked over to him and he immediately jumped to his feet, brushing himself off.

She pointed to the plants and he motioned toward the garden. They continued chatting for a few minutes. She reached out and gave him a hug and then proceeded to walk down the driveway toward the main road.

David glanced over his shoulder and saw me through the kitchen window. He stood for a moment, glaring at me, and then turned back to tending the garden. I wondered what they had spoken about. It wasn't the first time I felt that David already knew Conchita, the way they looked at each other, the way they conversed as if they were long-lost friends. If they already knew each other, why wouldn't he have told me? Could he be hiding something?

The door opened and David popped in, grabbing his keys off the counter.

"I'll be back in an hour," he said, wiping the sweat from his brow with the back of his hand.

"Where are you off to now?"

"Conchita just texted me. She missed the bus, so I offered to give her a ride home."

"What would she do without you?" The words spilling out of my mouth in a sarcastic tone.

"Seriously, Val?" He shot me a look and then slammed the door behind him.

That confirmed my suspicion. They did know each other. They had to have swapped phone numbers to be texting each other. What else were they keeping from me?

I waited until I heard David's truck roll along the gravel driveway and down toward the road. I marched over to the box next to the futon in the corner. Undoing the flaps, I reached in and pulled out the folder marked insurance—the one with my name on it.

I rifled through the papers but found most of them were written in Spanish. I had no clue about what they said. Tossing the file aside, I sat on the floor and gazed out the window. I stared at the trees, watching their leaves sway in the wind. The bright sun from the morning had disappeared as thick clouds were rolling in. It amazed me that the weather changed so quickly but it was the rainy season after all.

My mind wandered in a million directions as a chill crept over me. I somehow convinced myself that David had taken an insurance policy out on me. Why else would my name be on a folder marked insurance? I've heard stories before, read about them in the news, and watched them on TV—stories about a person who takes out an insurance plan on someone.

Someone they plan to kill.

24

David

I can't concentrate. I'm irritated. I am trying to connect the security camera to my phone but I don't have the head for it today. My thoughts keep drifting to Val.

I thought she was different, unlike the others. I thought she was more self-confident and secure. Once again, I was wrong. I caught her staring out the kitchen window when Conchita came out to say goodbye. I saw the look in her eyes. I've seen it before. The look of distrust fused with jealousy.

If she only knew what poor Conchita has endured. The guilt she feels and the burden she carries. Maybe it was a bad decision to return to Costa Rica. Perhaps I should've stayed in California. I could've saved myself time and energy… not to mention, money.

No. Screw that. I will not bend to another woman. You give them an inch, and they take a mile. My exes had the world at their feet but they threw it all away. It wasn't my fault. At least that's what I tell myself. One allowed herself to become caught up in the frivolities of the world. The other became entangled in delusions that diluted her mind. Sadly, she succumbed to her own fate.

I warned her many times that she was going down the wrong path. I tried stopping her. I tried even harder to steer her in the right direction but she wouldn't listen. She was too headstrong. Maybe she got what was coming to her.

Conchita thinks I should come clean and tell Val what happened. But I want to start new with a clean slate. I want to do things right this time, with the right woman. There's no use stirring up the past if you don't have to.

They say you shouldn't keep secrets but I beg to differ. Some secrets are best kept buried.

25

Valerie

As I sat at the computer staring at the screen, I pictured a sloth crossing the road. He was crawling along, carrying a power cord and searching for an electrical outlet. The internet connection at the house was slow, slower than the days of dial-up. Everything took forever; slow was the way of life in the jungle.

Ten minutes later the page appeared and I clicked on the link for batteries. Another two minutes passed and then the page froze. I released a long sigh. When I leaned back in the chair, I felt something grab my shoulders. Flinching, I let out a scream and turned in my seat.

"You scared me!" I shrieked my heart beating rapidly against my chest.

"The chair was balancing on two legs. It looked as if you were going to fall over, so I reached out to catch you."

I glared at him, taking a breath.

"What are you doing?" he asked, peeking at the screen.

"Trying to order a battery for my cell phone but I can't even get the darn page to load."

"Forget it. It's not worth it. The shipping will cost more than the battery. We can go into town and try to find one."

I wanted to tell him that I didn't like going into town. It was depressing to see the endless number of stray animals wandering aimlessly. It was so sad and always made me cry.

But for some reason, I didn't have the heart to tell him as he stood there holding my leopard print rain boots.

"Put these on; you might need them." He grinned.

Two hours and four stores later, there were no cell phone batteries to be found. I spied a BCR sign, a 'Banco de Costa Rica' on the main road and asked David to stop.

"I'll just be a minute," I said, exiting the truck. Digging into my handbag for my wallet, I pulled out my bank card.

As I walked up to the ATM, the 'cajero automático' I paused as everything was written in Spanish. Above the machine, the words 'sin cargos' were written on a small sign.

When I slid my card into the machine, I tapped the keypad and gazed into the screen, but the glare from the sun made it hard to read. Shielding my eyes from the sun, I tapped the keypad again. I must've hit the wrong button because in an instant the machine ate my card.

Stomping my feet, I grumbled and breathed out my frustration. A door slammed from behind me and David sauntered over with a goofy smile plastered on his face.

"What's going on?"

"The machine ate my card!" I yelled.

"Looked like you were doing some sort of rain dance." He broke into laughter. "At least you're wearing the right boots."

"Stop," I stamped my foot again, "it's not funny."

"Don't worry about it; things happen."

"But it's the only card I have."

"Relax," his tone escalated.

"Sure, easy for you to say." I rushed over to the main door, gripping the handle, but it was locked.

"They're closed," he said, "cerrado," pointing to the sign. "We'll come back another day."

"But I need money. Now."

"You don't need any money."

"I am out of cash." A wave of panic surged through me, pulsating every inch of my body.

"So what?" He walked over to me, inches from my face.

"What if I can't get my card back?"

"I'll take care of you," he said, staring deep into my

eyes. He took hold of my hand and we walked back to his truck.

The old jalopy chugged along, the springs in the seat squeaking as David dodged a mix of bumps and potholes in the road. I focused my gaze on a small waterfall streaming down the side of the mountain that reminded me of something I had seen before. Closing my eyes, I thought back to the waterfall photo in David's condo—to the time I first visited him in California.

I had so many hesitations when I first met him, yet I ignored every one of them. As we bounced along the winding roads, I glanced over at him, wondering if he had any doubts when he first met me.

"What are you thinking about over there?" he asked, reaching out for my hand.

"Not much," I turned away, gazing out the window.

"Don't lie; I can sense something is on your mind."

"I was thinking about the waterfall we just passed. It reminded me of the photo on the wall at your condo."

"Ahh, yes, the old condo. I had forgotten all about it since we moved here to our new home." He grinned, caressing my fingers. "What else is on your mind?"

I swallowed, shifting in my seat.

"Have you ever had second thoughts?" I asked, my voice wavering.

"About what?"

"Us," I said, over the faint beeping of his cell phone.

"No, why have you?" Drawing his phone from his pocket, he gazed at the screen squinting his eyes.

"No," I lied. "I guess because our relationship moved so fast, I've always wondered."

"Stop thinking so much and start enjoying yourself. We're living the dream life in the jungle." He gave me a wink.

When we pulled into the driveway, David parked the truck near the steps with the engine running. With his phone in hand, he began texting someone while I reached for my handbag and exited the vehicle. As I walked up the stairs toward the house, I heard gravel crunching as David turned the truck around.

"Slim needs my help," he called out. "I'll be back in a bit." He blew me a kiss and then drove back down the driveway.

I couldn't help wonder if it was really Slim or maybe Conchita who texted him. Max started barking and I immediately went over to greet him.

"Hello, my handsome boy," I said, untying him from the run. Jumping up and down, he ran circles around me and then dashed off in the direction of the garden.

I picked up my pace and followed him. I watched as he sniffed his way through the freshly planted flowers, stepping on some while leaving a trail of paw prints behind him.

"Max! Come over here," I yelled, patting my leg. I whistled at him but my attempt was weak. I never was a good whistler. Max soon started digging near a bright pink hibiscus as I slowly made my way toward him, step by step, ever so careful. Moving the soil with his paws and snout, Max unearthed something small and square. He tried clamping his jaw around it but it was too awkward for him. He began whining and then turned to me, wagging his tail.

"Whatcha got, boy?" I said as I moved closer. Max pawed at it before I picked it up, wiping the dirt from it. A small wooden box with the letter 'G' carved on top of it. I had no idea why it was buried there or what the letter G stood for.

I studied the box for a moment, feeling its weight and observing the tiny keyhole in the middle of it. I shook it by my ear but didn't hear any rattling inside. It felt solid.

I quickly placed the box back in its hiding place, patting the dirt around the plant to cover it up. I then made my way through the garden, backtracking over paw prints and footprints where Max and I trampled through the ground. I did my best to cover both of our tracks, smoothing the soil with the sides of my boots.

As I headed toward the house, I felt something soft brush against my shoulder, tickling my skin. I turned and saw a large plant with peach, bell-shaped flowers dangling from its stems. I took a step back to study it closer, noticing the heady, sweet aroma filling the air. The scent reminded me of something I couldn't quite put my finger on, a perfume maybe?

I continued down the path, and from a distance saw Max

sitting by the front door waiting for me. He had turned into such a great companion, loyal, smart, and obedient. When I reached the house, I patted Max on top of his head and then pulled the keys from my pocket to unlock the door.

My mind soon wandered, wondering where David had hidden the key to the wooden box in the garden.

26

David

I stand outside the kitchen window, watching Val as she riffles through the cardboard box, *my cardboard box.* She pulls out folder after folder, frantically scanning the papers inside each one. I feel my blood pressure rise as she intrudes into my personal life. What is she doing? What in the world could she be looking for?

Of course, she can't see me from this angle, not from where I'm standing. With the sun blazing bright in the afternoon sky, even if she were to look outside, the glare would blind her. It's like a big beaming spotlight shining inside the house and directly on her. *You're busted. We've caught you, the sun and I.* I chuckle to myself.

Val sits back on her heels, her eyes locked onto the piece of paper in her hand. With her finger, she traces over the lines on the page, one by one, until she reaches the end. Her mouth drops open as the paper falls from her hand and flutters to the floor. I gape as her hands fly up to cover her mouth to silence the scream she lets out.

As she turns her head toward the deck, I take a quick step back from the window, my foot catching on the leg of the wrought iron bench nearby. I fall to the ground with a loud thud and soon hear Max barking as he rushes over to the door. It opens.

"David! Are you okay?" Val stands frozen in the doorway, panic in her eyes.

"Yes," I say, slowly rising to my feet. I don't look at her as I brush the dirt and leaves from my jeans.

"What happened?" she asks, her voice trembling.

"I was just... uh," I wipe a bead of sweat from my forehead. "I was just moving the bench. It was too close to the house... too close to the window. I must have turned the wrong way and tripped over myself," I lie. I still don't look up as I walk past her into the house.

"What's going on here?" I ask, my eyes trailing to the cardboard box and papers strewn on the floor. Now it's my turn for questioning.

"Oh, I was just cleaning. Straightening up the house a bit," she says, her hands flitting in the air. "Max wanted to play ball, and when I tossed it, he ran and knocked over the box in the corner. I was in the middle of picking up the mess he made."

Well, well, well. She's *almost* a better liar than I am.

"Darling," I say, in my best syrupy sweet tone. "Why don't you boil some water? I'm in the mood for some tea."

Like the obedient girl she is, Val marches straight into the kitchen and turns on the faucet, filling the kettle. I sit at the table and watch as she strolls back to the living room to gather the papers that have fallen on the floor. I notice her thighs look a bit thicker than usual. She's gained some weight. We'll need to cut back on the cakes and cookies we've been enjoying lately. My craving for that coconut cream pie I saw at the bakery will have to wait.

The kettle whistles and she hurries over to the stove. She removes two cups from the cabinet and pours hot water into them. I study her as she reaches for the tin canister on the counter. When she opens it, she sighs.

"What's wrong?" I ask, even though I know the answer. "Are we out of tea?"

"Yes and no," she pouts. "We're out of green tea but we have some of that tea Conchita always brings with her."

"Great, I like hers better anyhow." I snicker.

"You do? I swear that stuff gives me weird dreams… and a headache."

"Well, it helps me sleep."

"For sure, it knocks me out."

"You'll get used to it. She's still perfecting her brew. I'll tell her to lighten up on a few herbs on the next batch."

Val grudgingly pulls two teabags from the canister and then slips one into each of the cups. She saunters over to me with cups in hand, placing them on the table.

Gazing at her, I bring the cup to my lips and take a long sip. She rolls her eyes, I'm guessing, at the slight sound that escapes my mouth.

"What?" I ask.

"Why do you always make that slurping sound when you drink?" She twists her lips and I detect a hint of disgust from the look on her face.

"Does it bother you?" I take another long sip, louder this time.

"Why do you answer me with a question?" Leaning back, she crosses her arms over her chest.

"Relax. Take another sip of your tea before it gets cold." I glare at her.

Val shakes her head and then reaches for her cup. She makes a loud sucking sound as she gulps down her tea, mocking me. Mid-swallow, she laughs, inhaling the liquid and starts choking. She coughs and coughs, squirming in her seat as she tries to remove the liquid from her lungs.

I jump up and rush to her side, knocking the chair backward. I position myself, ready to do the Heimlich Maneuver on her, but she stops me, putting a hand up in front of me.

"I'm okay," she says, her tone low and raspy. She takes in a shallow breath.

"You had me scared there for a moment."

"Serves me right." She clears her throat. "I shouldn't have made fun of you."

Bringing the cup to her nose, she inhales and then pauses. "That's weird," she says with a lilt in her voice.

"What now?"

"The smell," she scrunches her face as she sets the cup down.

"What smell?"

"The tea, the scent of that tea," she points. "I've smelled it somewhere before."

I tug at the string in my cup, lifting the teabag and take a quick whiff. "It smells a bit woody to me," I say, dangling it before placing it on the saucer.

"I think it smells like perfume. It has a sweet, floral aroma." She looks at me and yawns. I notice her eyes are glassy.

"You okay?" I reach over, stroking the back of her hand.

"Yeah, I feel tired all of a sudden."

"We've been up since dawn. Maybe you should take a little nap."

"I can barely keep my eyes open." She yawns again, half covering her mouth.

As she rises from the chair, she wobbles, unsteady on her feet. I reach up to grab hold of her arm as she collapses into me, falling onto my lap. She mumbles something but it comes out slurred. I have no idea what she's saying.

Draping her arm over my neck, I wrap my arm around her waist. I half walk, half drag her to the futon, lay her down, and prop a pillow behind her head. I unfold the blanket and cover her, tucking it up to her neck and behind her shoulders. She looks so peaceful, so snug. *Snug like a bug in a rug*, I silently laugh to myself.

I stand above her, watching her chest slowly heave up and down. She's the only woman I know who barely makes a sound when she breathes.

I remember the first night we slept together. I woke up and rolled over and thought she was dead. She was lying there motionless—pale faced and still as a statue. It didn't look as if she were breathing. The moment I placed my hand on her neck to feel for a pulse, she moved slightly and gasped for air. Even now, when I wake up in the middle of the night, I check to see if she's still alive.

I hear a whimper as she turns her head. Her eyes are still closed, but now she's facing me. I study her, watch as her lips twitch. I wait until her body goes limp. She's out like a light.

27

Valerie

The second I opened my eyes, I tried blinking away the stickiness inside my eyelids. Through blurred vision, I saw the ceiling fan whirling above me, its low hum streaming in my ears. I soon realized I was lying on the futon in the living room and not lying in our bed in the bedroom. *That's strange,* I thought.

Running my tongue over my lips, they felt chapped. My head hurt, my throat was dry, and my body was drenched in dampness. I was parched and sweating. My jeans and tank top were uncomfortably stuck to me. I wriggled around, my arms and legs flailing, battling an oversized piece of fleece with palm trees on it.

I stood up, flung the stupid blanket on the floor, and then made my way to the bathroom. Don't get me wrong, I love palm trees. Real ones, outside, where they belong with their leaves swaying in the wind. Planted, not printed loudly all over some cheap blanket.

I'll tell you, David has the worst taste in decor. I was beyond thankful when he asked me to help him decorate the place. I could not wait to replace most of the tacky-looking items he had purchased. He blamed his choices on limited selection, but I had no problem finding plain white towels and earth-toned curtains. You just had to look a little harder to find the good stuff. You had to go to more than one store and refuse to settle for less.

While I didn't remember falling asleep on the futon, I did remember my dream. Similar to the one I had had when I first arrived sans the dead body on the ground. Another dream of being trapped inside a house with no way out. This time, though, it felt so real. It was more vivid. It wasn't a dingy old shack but a quaint little house painted bright blue. The house sat in the middle of nowhere surrounded by tall, dense trees.

After a quick shower, I changed into some clean clothes and made my way to the kitchen. The smell of coffee wafted in the air and I spied a half pot on the coffee maker. As I reached for a mug, I noticed a piece of paper on the counter. It was folded in half with my name on it scribbled in blue ink. I opened it.

Hello Darling,

I hope you slept well. I missed you in our bed last night. I am out running a few errands and will be home in time for dinner.

Love you lots, David

Tossing the note aside, I filled my mug and padded toward the bedroom.

David's little note, the folded piece of paper, reminded me of another piece of paper I had found... in the box with the insurance papers. That one, however, was folded into squares. I prayed it was safely tucked away in the place I had stashed it.

I opened the clothes hamper, pulled out my jeans, shoving my hand in the back pocket. *Voila! Perfecto!* Thank goodness it was still there.

I carefully unfolded the paper, smoothing out the lines. After taking a sip of coffee, I placed the mug back on the nightstand and sat up in bed to reread it.

D,

I'm done. I can't do this anymore. All we ever do is argue and fight. Your promises, one after another, all broken and never kept. Why make a commitment you never intended to keep?

You built this house to be our oasis. You said it would be our safe haven. But it didn't turn out that way. Instead, it turned into a nightmare... a living hell.

Everything you brought into this house perished— flowers, plants, even my poor little fish. I swear it's the reason you brought me here. To trap me, to watch me shrivel up and fade away. To watch me suffer... to watch me die.

But know this.

I am not her. I never will be.

Therefore, it's time for me to leave.

I tried to make it work. I thought you would change. I actually thought I could change you. But who was I kidding? The only person being fooled was me.

When we first met, I was blinded. I had fallen madly in love... crazy, head-over-heels in love. I gave you my heart, but you tore it to pieces and stomped all over it.

"Trust me," you said. "You'll have to learn to trust me."

That's the thing about trust — it takes years to build and mere seconds to shatter.

You don't hurt the ones you love. You don't keep deep, dark secrets.

I'm sorry it has to end this way, but I've made my decision. Today is the day, the beginning of the end. My beginning and your end.

Today is the day I will be bound to you no more.

G

My hands shook slightly but not quite as bad as when I first read the letter. I'd had time to process things, to put two and two together. It was that moment when I knew. G was his ex-wife. And the box buried in the garden had something to do with her.

Was it a memory box? A collection of keepsakes? Or was it something else, something more sinister? Maybe he tried to stop her from leaving? Maybe something happened? Maybe he hurt her?

As my mind searched for answers, I couldn't help wonder. I wondered if she had been burnt and buried inside that box.

David

I pick up Val's phone and scroll through her contact list. A handful of names, mostly female, pass under my fingers, but I'm only looking for one. *Ahh, there she is.* I stop to study the number below her name. Slipping my phone from my pocket, I tap out the number and place it to my ear. She picks up on the third ring.

"Hello," she answers in a breathy tone.

"Hey, Cindy, it's David," I say, nonchalantly, not wanting to raise concern.

"David? David who?" she snips.

"Val's David, I am calling about Val."

"What's wrong? What happened? Is she okay?" She rapid-fires questions at me.

"Yes, she's okay. Listen, I'm a little concerned about a few things and wanted to talk to you. Do you have a minute?"

"What exactly are you concerned about?" she snaps. I picture her placing a hand on her hip.

"Well, she hasn't been herself lately," I rub the back of my neck, pausing for a second. "She seems sort of anxious and depressed."

"That doesn't sound like my Val," Cindy emphasizes the word 'my.'

"Maybe it's me. Maybe I'm projecting. I thought by now she'd be relaxed in her new home. I thought she'd be happy and content with the life I created for her."

"What do you mean the life you created for her? I don't understand." This time she emphasizes the word 'you.'

"Well, I hired a housekeeper… her name is Conchita. I figured she could help Val with chores, help her get acclimated and all."

Dead silence on the other end.

"Cindy? Hello? Are you still there?"

"Yeah, I am just wondering why you hired a housekeeper for a nine hundred something square foot house."

"It's different down here. It's not about the size of the house; it's about helping the community." I hesitate for a second. "Besides," I add, "Conchita is teaching Val to speak Spanish."

"You do know you can take lessons online these days. There's a bunch of sites that offer language courses free of charge."

"As I said, I enjoy helping the local community here. I'm providing a job to someone in need."

"So, has Val made any friends? Other than what's her name… Conchita?"

"No, she doesn't go out that often. She pretty much stays close to home but she does have Max."

"Max?"

"Our dog."

"Oh, that's right, Maximilian. She told me about him but I had forgotten his name." A long pause ensues before she pipes up again. "Hey, I have an idea."

"What's that?"

"I'll come down and visit. I'm sure that will cheer her up. I miss my Val and I desperately need a vacation from hotel hell."

I mute the phone to air my grievance. Honestly, I don't know what to say to her self-invitation. As I ponder the thought, I hear clicking sounds over the line as though someone is typing in the background. I unmute.

"So, I just checked the airlines and found a smoking deal. There's a flight that will put me there on Friday. I'm gonna grab it before it's gone."

"Sure, Cindy," I unwillingly relent, "go grab it and then text me your arrival time. I'll pick you up at the airport."

"I can take a cab if it's a bother."

"No, I don't want cabbies or strangers knowing where I live."

"Okay, then I don't want Val knowing that I'm coming down. I want it to be a surprise."

"Sure thing, Cindy, let's surprise her."

"Promise?"

"I promise," I sneer.

"See you on Friday," she squeals and ends the call.

I put Val's phone back in the exact place I found it next to the lamp on the nightstand where it is always setting. I keep telling her she shouldn't sleep with her phone by the bed. I read that it's not safe to be so close to your phone when you sleep—something about radiation and brain cancer. I really wish she'd listen to me more. It would be horrible if anything ever happened to my Val.

As I wander into the kitchen, I wonder if Cindy knows the size of other things in my life in addition to my house. Clenching my teeth, I can only imagine what Val tells her when they chit chat on the phone.

Val knows I'm a private guy. I don't like sharing information with people I don't know and don't want my dirty laundry aired. I tug on the refrigerator door and swipe a Ginger ale off the shelf. Pulling the tab, the soda hisses at me. I take a quick gulp, the bubbles tickling the back of my throat on their way down. I'm hopeful it will help soothe my sudden upset stomach.

While sipping my soda, I gaze around the house. I have no idea where Cindy is going to sleep when she arrives. With Val being the kindhearted gal she is, I'm sure she'll offer Cindy our bed. But if she thinks we're going to sleep on the futon in the living room, she's nuts. That thing is somewhere between a twin and a double. Maybe I'll sleep outside with Max in the doghouse. Nah, forget that idea. I'll sleep on the deck in the hammock under the stars.

I think back to when we took our little vacation to our last night as we strolled along the beach. The night I wished upon a shooting star and asked Val to do the same.

The wish I made that night miraculously seems to be coming true. My only hope is that I don't mess things up this time. Otherwise, it would be all for naught, a terrible waste.

29

Valerie

I hate playing games; I find them a complete waste of time. But I felt like I was involved in a murder mystery, a puzzle waiting to be solved. The puzzle pieces included insurance papers with my name on them, a box buried in the garden, and a handwritten letter from David's ex-wife. Well, one of his ex-wives... a probable missing or possibly dead ex-wife. I felt the hair rising on the back of my neck. *What other pieces of the puzzle was I missing?* I was determined to figure it out.

Marching into the living room, I headed straight for the box. Back to square one where I began. The key had to be hidden somewhere, maybe stashed away inside a file. I pictured

David's keychain and tried counting the number of keys on it from memory. *Too many*, I thought, shaking my head. But it would be the first and most logical place to keep a key.

I removed each and every folder, flipping them open, and searching inside. Nothing. There were no keys tucked away inside the box. Biting my lower lip, I sighed. Maybe I should have told him about my concerns. I had so many questions accumulating in my head that I was surprised they weren't spilling out my ears.

David hated being questioned and loathed confrontation. He easily became defensive and sometimes took things the wrong way, twisting them around. At times he even went as far as putting words in my mouth. That particular trait of his drove me batty.

I heard a tap on the window and glanced over and saw a yellow bird flapping its wings, hopping around in circles. Sliding the door open, I stepped out on the deck to make sure it was okay.

"Hello there, little one," I whispered, crouching down slowly beside it.

The bird chirped as it hopped around. I reached out calmly, my hand inches from it, curious if it would come near. At that moment, it tilted its head and looked up at me.

"Aren't you an adorable speckled fellow." I smiled. It took a tiny hop toward me and pecked at my hand.

"Aww, you must be looking for food. Some fruit, maybe?" Turning my head, I spotted some melon slices in the corner. "Oh good, David remembered to leave food out today."

I slowly walked over to the fruit, hoping the little bird would follow me. Sure enough, it soared right over my head, landing and then perching by the edge of the deck. I watched as it pecked at the melon for a few minutes. With a full belly, the bird looked up at me as if to say thanks and flew away.

I hung out on the deck for a while, not wanting to go back inside. I spent many days being cooped up in that house and felt like a prisoner at times. David was gone a lot; he was always leaving me alone. Well, not all alone; I have Max. And I don't know what I would have done without him.

Other than the humidity, it was a gorgeous day. The sun peeked through the trees and a gentle breeze swayed the leaves. I had decided to try the new hammock David had bought. After our vacation at The Green Tree House, it was all he ever talked about.

When we spotted one on a shopping trip to town, his eyes lit up. As soon as we returned home, he immediately wanted to tie it between two trees but instead, I suggested we buy a stand for it. Of course, there wasn't a store that sold hammock stands, so David the handyman built one.

Sinking into the thick woven fabric, I swayed side to side until I found my balance. I lay perfectly still, losing myself in the songs of the jungle—the trilling of the birds, the low buzzing of insects, and the squawking somewhere off in the distance.

As I closed my eyes, I heard a disturbing grunting sound. I froze, my hands gripping the hammock tight on both sides as a loud scream echoed through the air. Scrambling, I tipped over in the hammock and fell flat on my face. Then a second scream, louder with a screeching yelp.

I sat back on the deck, pulling my knees to my chest. There was a low growling and then a long string of howling. Max? No! Max! My heart dropped to my stomach.

I jumped up and took off sprinting as fast as I could through the house to the front door, swinging it open. Another scream flooded my ears—a guttural, blood-curdling scream.

30

David

I make my way up the walkway carrying a statue I bought, trying to decide where to put it. As I get closer to the house, I glance over and see Val sitting by the front door. Max is there lying beside her. She's stroking his fur with one hand and wiping her eyes with the other. I immediately set the statue on the ground and rush to her side.

"Val, what's going on? Are you okay? Is Max okay?" My eyes dart to her face, to Max, and then back to her.

"Yes, thank goodness. I thought something happened to him, something terrible," her voice raw. Her face is streaked with tears and she's all stuffed up.

"What do you mean something terrible? What the—?"

"Oh, David, I heard this horrible screaming." Her eyes widen. "I have no idea where or who it was coming from. I've never heard anything like it."

"Can you describe it? What did it sound like?"

"It was so weird and scary. Like a growling and grunting and then a hollering... all at the same time."

"Sounds like the howlers."

"Howlers?"

"Yes, the howler monkeys. You just described them to a T."

"Whatever they were, they were beyond frightening." Her shoulders twitch.

"My ex-wife was terrified of... " I catch myself starting to say. Val gazes up at me but I shake my head. "Never mind," I stop myself and remain silent.

Max stands up, interrupting us, and starts licking her tears.

I watch as he kisses her face. I can't remember the last time we kissed, Val and I, not the dog. I've been so busy with the house and all. She was so upset when I missed our dinner the other night. But what can I say, the day got away from me. She must realize things are slower here and don't move as quickly as they do in the states. Work matters take longer, sometimes weeks or even months to complete. But no excuses. We definitely need to spend more time together.

I walk back over to the statue and pick it up to show Val.

"What do you think?" I ask, cradling it. "Do you like it?"

"What is it? A bird?"

I turn it around to show her the front. "No, it's an angel."

She sits there staring, first at the statue and then at me, not saying a word. She's deep in thought and I wonder what she's thinking.

We go inside and I pull a bottle of wine off the rack I built. Opening it, I take two glasses from the cabinet and pour the wine, handing a glass to Val.

"Thanks," she says. I'll start dinner. "Is spaghetti okay?"

"Sure." Reaching for the wine, I study the dark liquid as it swirls in the glass. A vision flashes before my eyes and I shut them tight, forcing the scene away—that horrific, bloody, tragic scene. One I hope and pray I never see again.

I inhale deeply and then take a sip. I need to put my old life behind me and focus on the new one I've created. *Out with the old and in with the new,* I tell myself. I take another breath and repeat the mantra a few more times.

I stroll into the living room and plop down on the futon, putting my feet up on the coffee table. Val hates it when I do that, but what the hey, I bought it. She also hates the table and says it doesn't go with the decor. She tells me every day but I ignore her.

I'm about function and utility, not style. Why do they call it a coffee table anyway? I mean, at the moment, there's no coffee, only an array of other things on it: a magazine, a glass of wine, and one of her vanilla-scented candles. I'd say it's an anything and everything table, including a footrest. I reach for my drink, having a little laugh to myself.

After a heaping bowl of pasta, I lean over and give her a peck on the cheek. She pulls away, rubbing her forehead.

"You okay?" I gently massage her shoulder.

"I have a headache. It's been a long day."

"I'll clean up, you go lie down."

"Thanks." She half smiles. She stands up from the table and heads for the bedroom, closing the door.

After doing the dishes, I pour myself another glass of wine and mosey over to the desk I made. Val needed a place to do her writing, so I thought I'd build her a little writing desk. She designed it and picked out the wood, teak. It's nothing fancy but it seems to fit perfectly in the corner.

She thanked me for it, calling me 'crafty' and I knew what she meant. I've been called worse before.

I take a seat and flip open the computer. I have some research to do. My laptop is in the bedroom, but I don't want to go in there and wake Val. I'm sure she won't mind if I use her new computer since I'm the one who bought it.

As I click through the sites and scroll down the pages, I think about opening up to Val. I consider telling her about my past and about my ex-wives. I contemplate telling her everything, even what happened on that fateful day.

Conchita has been pestering me about it once again. She says I should, 'confesarse.' Or in English, 'come clean,' 'confess.'

It's such a crazy, unbelievable tale. Where would I begin?

Valerie

Those three words, 'ex-wife,' 'no,' and 'angel.' I'd heard them before.

I thought back to when we first arrived in Costa Rica and I overheard Slim talking to David in the casita and the strange look he gave me. I wished I had heard the entire conversation to make sense of it all but I didn't. So it became another piece of the puzzle.

Staring at the computer screen, I waited for the site to load—the background information site where I saw a photo of a woman named Susan. When the page appeared, all the data had disappeared along with the picture. I searched for more information on David, hoping to find a link to a name with the letter 'G' but came up empty.

Since I had hit a dead-end, I decided to send Cindy an email as it had been weeks since we last spoke. After composing a quick message, I went up to the toolbar to insert an emoji. As the cursor arrow drifted by the history tab, a long list of recently searched phrases appeared, but they weren't mine.

David must have used my computer and forgot to clear his search history.

Pausing for a moment, I quickly scanned the words, hoping they might help me solve the puzzle. Most of the searches were for teas, herbs, and flowers. One certain phrase, however, caught my eye. It more than stood out; it screamed out, sending shivers up my spine. I blinked rapidly, unsure of what I saw.

Two words read 'deadly concoctions.'

My mind raced in a million directions. I felt weak as I gripped the sides of the chair, trying to catch my breath. I deep breathed so I wouldn't pass out and kept telling myself to stay calm.

Minutes later, the front door opened and David appeared. I saw grocery bags hanging from his arms and someone hiding behind him. I knew it wasn't Conchita because the long, bare legs behind him didn't belong to her; they belonged to someone else I knew. When he walked inside, placing the bags on the counter, she stood in the doorway smiling at me.

Cindy.

"Look what the cat dragged in," he said with a sweeping wave of his hand.

Cindy elbowed him, "You must be the cat."

I was at a complete loss for words.

"Val," she squealed. "What's wrong? You look like you've seen a ghost." She came rushing over to me.

"What are you? How are you? How did you get here?" I stammered.

"A plane, silly," she snorted. "How else do you think I got here? Then again, I suppose I could've sailed here in a boat." She remarked, winking at David.

"I'm surprised you're here," I said. Steadying myself, I rose from the chair.

"Happy to hear; that was the plan." She grinned and gave me a hug.

"The plan," I stepped back, glaring at David. "What plan?"

"To surprise you," she tugged on my arm. "I wanted it, or rather me, to be a surprise."

"Who planned this?" I asked, my eyes flicking between the two.

"Is there a problem?" David sighed, glancing at me. I watched as he stood in the kitchen, placing three new bottles of wine on the rack. Crumpling the paper bag, he tossed it in the trash and then unpacked more groceries.

"I see you did a little shopping while you were out," I walked over to help him put the items away.

"My fault," Cindy butted in. "I made him stop. I want to make dinner for you guys tonight; it's the least I can do for letting me stay here."

David rolled his eyes as he opened the fridge. He pulled out two bottles of water and handed one to Cindy.

"Thanks. I'm sooo thirsty."

"So, Cindy tells me she makes a mean taco salad," David said. Twisting off the cap, he chugged half the bottle.

"What else did she tell you?" I didn't make eye contact with David as I closed the cabinet. "I'm guessing you picked her up at the airport."

"Yep, he did." Cindy chimed in. "We talked about a lot of things, didn't we?"

"You'll have to fill me in." Opening the fridge, I retrieved a bottle of water since David forgot me when doling them out.

"I'm off. I have things to do. You two are on your own for the rest of the day." As he walked past, he gave me a quick peck on the cheek and headed out the door.

"Show me the views." Cindy grabbed my hand, pulling me toward the glass doors. I slid one open and we stepped outside.

"This house," she gazed all around. "The set up is way too cool. You must love living here." Strolling to the end of the deck, she peered over the edge.

"Be careful, please. David still needs to put up the railing."

A parrot flew by landing in a tree in front of us. "Val," she pointed. "Look at that bird. He's amazing!"

"Yeah, and they are pretty friendly too. We feed them every day." I tromped over to a banana peel and picked it up, flinging it in the yard.

Cindy walked back to me and made a sad face, draping an arm around my shoulder.

"Honey, what's wrong? You don't seem like yourself."

"I don't know… things haven't been going so well."

"Have you been writing? How are the books coming along?"

"No books, I've been too busy piecing things together."

"Huh?"

"I'm trying to solve a puzzle."

"Puzzle? What are you talking about?"

"This place," I said, waving my arm. "It's become one big mystery." I turned and walked toward the door.

"What do you mean? I don't understand," she followed me back inside and we sat on the futon.

Leaning forward, I rested my elbows on my knees and blew out a long slow breath. "I don't even know where to start."

"The beginning would be a good place," she said, brushing the hair from my face. "You seemed so happy when you first arrived here."

"Yeah," I sat back and began counting on my fingers. "That was before the ATM ate my card and before I saw life insurance papers with my name on them. Before I found a wooden box buried in the garden and before finding a strange letter from his ex-wife who, according to Slim, I resemble."

"Gosh! That does sound like a mystery," she faltered. "Who's Slim?"

"A friend of David's who picked us up at the airport."

"Oh, well, now that I'm here, we can solve the puzzle together."

I sighed, shrugging my shoulders.

"Look on the bright side; at least you have a dog."

"Yeah, my one true friend around here, my loyal companion."

Cindy made the sad face again. "I was wondering why you weren't happy to see me when I walked in the door."

"Sorry, it has nothing to do with you. Right before you got here, I was on the computer and happened to see David's search history." I frowned.

Her eyes widened. "Uh-oh, what did you find?"

"It's what I saw."

"Let me guess," she raised an eyebrow, "an email from another woman?"

"No," I snapped, "a phrase, a search term." I chewed on my thumbnail.

"So, what then? Tell me. What did it say?"

"Deadly concoctions." I trembled, feeling my heart race as the words left my mouth.

"What the hell?" She scooted over, placing her hand on my shoulder. "Why on earth would David be searching for such things?"

"I have no idea but mark my words, I will find out."

David

I walk into the house and the sweet scent of vanilla hits me in the face. A vase of hand-picked flowers, from my garden by the looks of them, sits in the middle of the table. Next to it, a white, flickering candle, wax dripping down the side into a small hardened pool on the table. Reaching for a butter knife, I gently scratch it off, hoping it doesn't leave a stain on the wood. As I take a step back, rolling the wax into a tiny ball, I study the arrangement for our guest.

A table set for three.

Off in the distance, I hear voices and the clinking of glasses. Then a burst of laughter and a door sliding open and closed. I gaze over and there they are heading my way.

Yin and Yang.

Cindy, making herself right at home, grabs a bottle of wine on the counter and refills their glasses.

"Care for one?" she asks, gripping the bottle by its neck, waving it in the air.

I want to say, 'yes' to her offer as an entire bottle of wine is exactly what I need to deal with Cindy, Ms. Yin, this evening. I anticipate a night of antics, a tawdry replay of our boozy dinner in LA. Instead, I flash her a smile, shake my head, and decide to start with a glass.

I reach to the rack for a bottle of red, open it, and fill my glass halfway. Swirling the wine, I then raise the glass to my lips, inhaling the vapors.

"You're not one of *those*, are you?" Cindy quips.

"One of those?" I inquire sarcastically. I take another sip.

"He is," Val interjects. "Not only is he a 'swirler' but he's also a 'questioner.'"

"I see," Cindy says, eyeballing me and then flicking her gaze to Val. "But we're used to guys like him, aren't we V?" She elbows Val.

I glare at them. "A little inside joke, hmm?"

Cindy overly swirls her glass, mocking me. "Relax, we deal with swirlers and questioners all the time at the hotel." She giggles. Val blushes and gazes down, shaking her head. "Correction," she nudges Val, "in Val's case, the word is dealt. She's dealt with your kind before," she slightly slurs, pointing at me. "I, on the other hand, still do," she points to herself. "I still deal with them."

Here we go, let the Cindy games begin. She's already tipsy and stumbling over her words. I let out a loud breath.

"It's dinner time," I announce. "Let's eat." I pull out a chair and take a seat. Cindy follows suit.

Val removes the taco salad from the fridge and divides it among three plates. She then waltzes over and does a little bunny dip as she places each dish on the table. They must have taught her that move at the hotel, in Etiquette 101—how to properly serve guests. I like it; it works. I also admire that she can carry three plates on one arm so effortlessly and not drop one.

I devour a considerable portion of the salad and compliment Cindy on her cooking skills. Believe it or not, it's hard to find decent Mexican food here. I've been telling Slim that he needs to open a restaurant. He's always looking for new business ideas and he knows half the people in town. But it all comes down to time and money as it always does, and of course, finding good help. The rules are quite different here. Starting a business is not easy and requires copious amounts of patience.

After dinner, Val retrieves a covered dish from the counter and places it in the middle of the table. When she removes the tin foil, we all gawk in unison.

"What are they?" Cindy says, sliding a long red fingernail under one, lifting it by its corner.

"Pineapple empanadas," Val sulks. She looks as deflated

as the dessert sitting in front of us.

"That's right; I remember having them one time. They looked different, though, more doughy and pillowy." Cindy pinches it between her fingers and takes a bite. Pineapple oozes out and onto her plate.

"Yeah, they fell flat." Val frowns. "I swear it must be the humidity here. Nothing I make comes out right."

I don't want to add salt to the wound, but let's face the facts. Val is a much better preparer than baker. The poor gal can't cook to save her life. I reach for one and bite into it, pretending to enjoy it.

"Delicious," I say, forcing another bite. Listen, if I'm going to indulge in a sweet treat, it better be good, darn good. I refuse to waste calories on tasteless creations.

"Hey, have you guys ever had that spongy, milky cake?" Cindy asks. "I forget what it's called. I think it has whipped cream on top."

"Tres leches," I say, gazing at Val. "We had it on vacation, remember?"

"Yeah, it was so yummy. It can't be that hard to make but I'm sure I'd mess it up."

"Aww, V. Don't be so hard on yourself. I'll help you with it; we can make it together tomorrow," Cindy looks over, winking at me and Val catches her in the act.

"What's going on?" Val snaps, crossing her arms over her chest.

"Nothing," I say, shaking my head.

"Cindy, I saw you wink at him."

"It wasn't the first time," I say, giving Cindy the side eye.

Suddenly I feel a kick from under the table and reach down to massage my shin. "She winked at me earlier when she first arrived."

The chair scrapes against the floor as Val jumps up. She throws open the cabinet, grabs the bag of dog food, and fills Max's bowl. With bowl in hand, she stomps out the front door, slamming it behind her.

"What are you doing?" Cindy reprimands me.

"What do you mean, what am *I* doing? What are *you* doing?" I glare. "I know it was you who winked at me. CutieC, how original," I scoff, rolling my eyes.

"Oh please, I knew it was you, too. I was testing you," she hisses.

"Testing me? For what?"

"To see if you were good enough for my friend." She pushes back from the table and tromps into the living room.

"Who are you to judge?" I sneer. "Of course, I'm good enough." Picking up my glass, I rise from the chair. "I'm the best thing that's happened to her."

"Then why the hell are you keeping her locked up from everyone?" she rages.

"Are you out of your mind? I'm not locking her up." I take a step closer. "Did Val say that?" I watch Cindy's mouth drop as she looks past my shoulder.

"Did Val say what?" I turn and see Val standing in the doorway, hands on her hips, staring at me.

Valerie

None of us slept much that night. David stormed off and fell asleep outside in the hammock. I had offered Cindy our bed but she insisted on sleeping on the futon. She felt bad about what had happened at dinner and kept apologizing, blaming herself for our petty quarrel. David, of course, blamed it on her and the alcohol. How quickly he forgets the times when he's had a few too many drinks. He forgets when he's made a scene, created unnecessary drama, and caused me heartache. I can't even begin to tell you how many times he's blatantly flirted with women right in front of my eyes. There were so many that I have lost count.

I shouldn't have become upset when Cindy winked at

him. I know how flirtatious she can be at times. She completely opened up and was honest with me, telling me everything over coffee the next morning.

"You know I only winked at him to see if he'd wink back, right?" she pleaded, sitting on the counter, her long legs dangling.

"What if he had winked back, then what?" I held the mug tight in my hands.

"But he didn't," she stated, hopping off the counter, her bare feet slapping the tile. "Besides, he hadn't logged into the site in months. You can see a person's last activity on their profile, you know."

"No, I wouldn't know. I don't do dating sites."

"So when David called me—"

"How did he get your number?"

"Gosh, V, I don't know. He probably got it from your phone."

"Great, so now he's looking at my phone."

"Seriously? You've been snooping through his files and digging in the garden... you're not exactly innocent, you know."

"Fair enough, continue."

"Listen, he's concerned about you. When he first told me you weren't acting like yourself, I didn't believe him. But now I see what he means. You're all edgy."

"And I have every right to be, considering what's been going on."

"David thinks you're anxious or depressed… or maybe both."

"So, did he invite you here to check on me or diagnose me?"

"Oh, stop it, Val, c'mon now, I invited myself. I was worried about you. I offered to take a cab, but he insisted on picking me up at the airport."

"What else did he say about me? What else did you talk about?"

"Not much… just the dog and the housekeeper, what's her name?"

"Conchita," I sighed. "Actually, she should be here any minute. David told me she's coming by today to bring more tea."

"Tea? What kind of tea?"

"She makes this special homemade brew."

"Is it any good? What does it taste like?"

"It's sort of bitter and smells like floral perfume. It's like a chamomile tea and it's supposed to calm you."

"Sounds interesting."

"I don't like it, but David's all into it. It knocks me out and gives me wacky dreams. I've only had it twice but I hate the way I feel after I drink it."

"Hmm, it kinda sounds like that ayahuasca stuff."

"Aa-yuh-waa-skuh?" I giggled. "What's that? I can't even pronounce it."

"It's some type of plant that grows in the rainforest.

They brew it to make a hallucinogenic tea and people travel to the jungle, to places like this, to drink it. They have whole ceremonies around it."

"Really? How do you know about it? Have you tried it?"

"No, a friend of mine has. He said it smells and tastes like crap."

"What else is in it?"

"I don't know exactly but supposedly it makes you puke your guts out and sends you on a wild and crazy psychedelic trip."

"Eww gross. That sounds like loads of fun."

"Not!" She bent over and made a loud hacking sound. We burst out laughing.

"Okay, enough of that; want more coffee?" she asked, swiping my empty mug from the table.

"Sure."

Cindy went over and grabbed the coffee pot and poured us each a second cup. As she turned around, she paused and looked out the kitchen window. She stood in front of it for a moment, gazing toward the garden.

"Hey, there's a woman out there with David. She's got long black braided hair... she's carrying a burlap bag."

"That would be Ms. Conchita."

"Cool purple dress she's wearing."

"What's David doing?" I asked, glancing over at her.

Stretching her neck, she leaned in closer to the window.

"He's kneeling on the ground next to what looks like a small statue."

"So, that's where he's putting it," I muttered.

"What did you just say?" She padded over, placing my mug back in front of me.

"I think his ex-wife is buried in the garden."

"What?" she gasped, spilling her coffee on her white tank top. Tugging on her shirt, she wiped at it. "Dang it, I think I just ruined this top. It's my favorite," she moaned.

"That wooden box I told you I found. Well, actually, I didn't find it; Max did. He sniffed it out and dug it up."

"What about the box and his wife?" She went over to the sink, turning on the faucet and dabbed her shirt with water.

"I have a feeling the box has something to do with his ex-wife. Maybe her ashes are stored in it. Why else would he keep a box locked up and buried?"

"Hmm... not sure, but I guess that would make sense."

"Especially since he bought a statue of an angel and put it in the garden."

"But are you sure she's dead? What's his wife's name? Or what was her name?"

"Which one?" I tilted my head.

"What do you mean which one?" She narrowed her eyes.

"He has two ex-wives," I said, holding up my fingers.

"Has or had?" she questioned. "Maybe they're both dead," her eyes went wide.

There was a knock on the door and Cindy walked over to open it. There stood Conchita, smiling at me, waiting to be invited inside. She was so demure and always polite.

"Hola. Pase por favor." I smiled, waving her into the kitchen. She ambled toward me and took a seat at the table. Reaching into her bag, she pulled out five cotton sacks of teabags.

"Estos son nuevos," she spoke softly, pushing them near me.

"New," Cindy said, sitting down to join us. "She said they're new." Picking up a sack, she dug a fingernail inside it and pulled out a teabag.

"I know what she said," I remarked. "I've been studying my Spanish."

Conchita looked down and away as if I had just said something about her.

"Val me dijo que haces esto," Cindy said and then turned to me. "I just said that you told me she makes this."

"Sí, es casero," Conchita replied. Cindy translated for me again. "Yes, it's homemade."

"¿Cual es el nombre?" Cindy continued. "What is the name?"

Cindy was all chipper. I watched as she talked with her hands, acting like Conchita's new best friend.

"Despierta," Conchita replied, beaming at Cindy. She showed her the tag at the end of the string and pointed to the word written on it.

"Desperate?" I asked, leaning over trying to decipher it. My eyes met Cindy's and we both shrugged our shoulders.

Neither of us knew what Conchita had said as she sat there smiling at us.

David

The evening is off to a great start. I promised myself tonight would be a much better one than last evening. Cindy whipped up an insanely delicious grande-sized pan of tres leches. It is light, luscious, and airy... just like her.

Oh, come on, don't hate. I'm a man. Besides, I've already mentioned it is okay to look as long as you don't touch. What's that saying? No harm, no foul. Show me a man who wouldn't look twice at a cute blonde with tan, toned legs in a pair of short shorts. You couldn't, could you? I'm right again, aren't I? I love it when I'm right.

I lick the last of the cream from my fork and think of indulging in a second slice but then I run a hand over my protruding belly and decide to pass. Instead, I swill the last of my wine, set the glass down, and stroll over to the TV. Seizing the remote, I scroll through the music channels, settling on Val's favorite era, the eighties.

Although she was just a child in that decade, it seems pop songs are her favorite. I sometimes hear her playing that type of music when she's doing her workout routine and since we both need to increase our exercise regime, the eighties it is.

I start swaying my hips to some hair metal song I can't name. The eighties, unfortunately, were just a blur to me. Back then, I was too busy trying to survive, working two jobs and hustling for a buck.

Cindy drifts past me, grooving to the music, a bottle of white in one hand and two long-stemmed glasses dangling from the other.

"Are you going to join us on the deck?" she asks as she spins around, heading out the doorway.

"Why not," I reply.

"Then grab a glass," she says, glancing over her shoulder.

I stride into the kitchen and open a bottle of red, refilling my glass. Sipping it, I head outside to join the ladies under the stars.

I have to admit, it is kind of fun having Cindy around, someone who gets my crass humor and who's not so serious. She's not sensitive and uptight like Val. That woman can be so emotional and boring at times.

I sometimes miss those wanton days, lusting after women like Cindy. The good for a day, better for a night, and best when you leave them in the morning type of gals.

Taking a long sip of wine, I tell myself to stop. It's not me, it's not who I am anymore. It's the wine working its wicked way through my veins. Such a sinful spirit it is.

I take a seat next to Val at our new bamboo dining set with different colored chairs, two green and two yellow. It seems to be the style these days. Val fell in love with the set the second she saw it, so I bought it for her. The only time she seems content is when she busies herself with decorating. We all have our little hobbies we enjoy.

I look at her sitting there quietly in a yellow chair while noticing my chair is green. Gripping her wine glass, she gives me a lopsided grin. At times I wonder if we're suited for each other or are we, once again, just another mismatch.

I don't think Val likes my style. It's okay, most women don't. It's more of what you might call an acquired taste. My last wife called it cheesy. No, that wasn't it. Oh, what was the word? Let me think for a moment… chintzy. Yes, that's the word; it's precisely what she used to say every time I showed her something I liked.

But David, it's so not me, it's so chintzy. I picture her overdrawn hot pink lips yakking away. Her constant drivel drove me bonkers.

Cindy snaps me out of my self-wallowing pity party—literally. I gaze up and there she is, snapping her pointy-nailed fingers in front of my face. She could slice salami with those talons.

"David, did you hear me?" She appears slightly irked.

"No, what did you say?" I cup my ear.

"I said what's up with your friend Conchita and her tea?" Wine spills from her glass as she takes a forceful swig.

"She makes homemade tea."

"Uh, duh. Tell me something I don't know," she rolls her eyes.

"She has a garden full of flowers and herbs. She enjoys making different blends of tea."

"Well, whatever she's mixing up is giving Val nightmares and making her sick."

"I know, Val has told me the way she feels after drinking the tea. Conchita needs to rebalance the blend. I've been helping her with it; we're trying to get the formula right."

"What formula? The one for her new desperate tea?" She cackles.

"Desperate?" I ask. I think Cindy's confused.

"What did she call that new tea she brought over earlier?" She looks over at Val.

"Something like the word desperada or desperado... I'm not sure of the pronunciation," Val replies.

"Despierta," I say. The word is despierta."

"What does it mean?" Cindy asks.

"Awake."

"So, she has tea to make you sleep and now tea to keep

you awake." She rolls her eyes again. "How convenient is that?"

"It's not what you think," I hesitate. "It's a different kind of awake."

Cindy pauses and peers at Val and they exchange a funny look.

Running a hand through my hair, I let out a breath. I am not in the mood to go there tonight. The 'awake' tea is not something you can explain to someone when their thoughts are clouded. The first rule of being awake is being pure and clean, cleansed from all distractions. Alcohol does the complete opposite; it taints the mind. They're not ready to receive the message and I'm not sure if they ever will be.

"Fess up David, what's going on here?" Val demands. "You're never around. I feel like I'm in the dark about everything."

"That wine has made you quite fearless," I say, holding her gaze.

"Liquid wisdom," Cindy says and then bursts out laughing.

"The true beverage is tea... not wine," I correct her. "Tea is liquid wisdom." I ponder for a moment while scratching my chin. "Thank you, Cindy. You just gave me a brilliant idea."

They both turn and give me the evil eye.

"I think I'll use that name for our new company."

"What new company?" Val asks bemused.

"I was going to surprise you, but it's impossible to keep a secret around here."

"It's not good to keep secrets in relationships," Cindy yaps. "Haven't you heard?"

"Conchita and I are going into business together," I announce, hoping they'll shut their mouths for a moment.

"Doing what?" Val asks.

"Selling tea?" Cindy guesses.

"Correct." I point to Cindy. "We're going to sell tea, homegrown, specialty-brewed tea. 'Liquid Wisdom' is the perfect name for it."

"Well, glad I could help," Cindy waves a hand through the air and saunters away.

Val stares at her empty wine glass looking dejected. Scooting my chair closer, I wrap my arm around her shoulder.

"I was going to tell you, but I wanted it to be the right time," my voice is sympathetic. She pulls away. She won't look at me. "I wanted to have all the teas properly blended. I promise I was going to tell you when we were closer to launching the business." Sliding her chair back, she stands up and walks into the house after Cindy.

I thought I'd have a moment to gather my thoughts, but one of them decides to increase the volume on the TV. The music is blaring and my house sounds like a discotheque.

I gaze through the glass door and see them hugging. Cindy pulls back, holding Val's hands and soon they're dancing in the living room. All that's missing is a mirrored disco ball hanging from the ceiling. I envision a globe dangling and shining, adding a little sparkle to the place. Women like sparkle, I know for a fact. My last wife bedazzled everything she got her greedy little hands on, hats, jackets, shoes… everything except me.

Here come the gals, side-by-side, back through the door and out onto the deck. They're jumping around and pointing to each other, singing along to the song that's playing. It's a catchy tune, but I've never heard it before.

I listen more carefully and try following the lyrics. Something about a 'cocktail bar and working as a waitress.' I can see why they like this song. I met Val in a cocktail bar when she was working as a waitress.

Tapping my feet, I smile and continue to listen. 'Picking you up and turning you around.' Yep, exactly what I did for my Val. I picked her up and turned her life around.

Now they're bopping and circling each other, really getting into it. They each sing a line and then laugh out loud.

The mood has certainly lightened, and I can't help but laugh along with them. They both turn and point to me, belting out the words.

"Don't you want me, baby?"

Jumping out of my chair, I shimmy over to Val, showing her my best dance moves.

"Hey, you guys, this is your song!" Cindy yells, wedging herself between us. She slips one arm around me, and one arm around Val, turning us into a Cindy sandwich.

"Could these lyrics be any more true?" Cindy shouts. She soon breaks away from us.

I watch as she bounces over to the end of the deck. The song is still playing and I see her teetering too close to the edge. The vision flashes before my eyes and I shut them tight, forcing the sight away. That horrific, bloody, tragic scene. *Will it ever go away?*

When I open my eyes, Cindy's arms are flailing and she's balancing on one foot. I sprint into action and rush over to grab her. She twists to the side as her leg gives way mere seconds from falling off the deck.

Valerie

"How's your ankle?" I asked Cindy as she sat on the floor, massaging her leg.

"It's a little sore," she grimaced. "I'm thankful I didn't break anything."

"I can't believe you almost fell off the deck last night."

"Yeah, all that dancing and wine…"

"Too much wine once again."

"It was all in good fun." She smirked.

"You should've seen the look on David's face when he grabbed you. He turned white as a sheet. I've never seen anyone so terrified."

"Probably because of the huge rock on the ground, right

below where I was standing. Gosh, Val, can you imagine if I fell on that thing? I could have cracked my head wide open," she quivered.

"I know," I replied. But I can't help thinking his reaction was due to something else. He looked almost grief stricken.

Wiggling her toes, Cindy adjusted the bandage wrapped around her ankle. "I feel so bad going through his personal things. I mean, the man just saved my life."

"But you promised to help me solve this puzzle."

"I know I did, but are you sure about all of this? About the—"

"You have to believe me. I'll show you. I know it's in here somewhere."

We sat in the living room digging inside David's box. I needed to show Cindy the papers I found with my name on them, proof of the insurance plan he had taken out on me. She watched as I flipped through each and every file, but the folder was nowhere to be found.

"It's not here… it's gone." Sitting back on my heels, I frowned.

"Maybe you didn't see or read it right. C'mon Val, you can barely speak, let alone read Spanish."

"Okay, okay, just help me put the files back then." I huffed, feeling defeated. "I'll show you the wooden box. I know exactly where it is."

"Whatever," she shook her head.

We trudged outside and into the garden, Cindy limping

behind me. Since her shoe size was smaller than mine, my rain boots fit perfectly over her bandaged ankle.

When Cindy first twisted her ankle, she kept moaning in pain. David had offered to take her to the hospital for an x-ray to make sure it wasn't fractured but she whined about not trusting the doctors in a third world country. As much as David consoled her, assuring she would be adequately cared for, she declined. Having had many sprained ankles in his past, he knew what to do and was kind enough to attend to her needs. Thankfully he had a first aid kit tucked under the bathroom sink. He said you should always be prepared for the unexpected.

I stood at the edge of the garden, scratching my head, bewildered. There were bright pink hibiscus plants scattered throughout. Last week there had been only one.

"What's the matter?" Cindy asked, hobbling over to me.

"David planted a whole bunch of new flowers," I said, walking over to the other side where I counted ten pink hibiscus plants. "I'll have to dig them all up to find it," I sighed in frustration. "Maybe Max can help me sniff it out. I'll go untie him; he was the one who found it last time." I headed toward the dog run.

"Stop, Val. I don't want to do this anymore," Cindy shrieked.

I turned around and walked back over to her. "What's wrong?"

"Seriously?" she shouted. "What's wrong with you?" Her eyes filled with tears.

I had no idea what caused the sudden change in her.

"Look at this place," she stumbled, hopping on one foot. "You live in paradise." She paused for a second, catching her breath. "And that house," she pointed, "the glass house." She gimped closer to me. "Some people would kill to live in a house like that in a place like this."

I stood silent as she threw her hissy fit at me. Staring at the ground, I bit down on the inside of my cheek. She had no idea what came with a house like that in a place like the jungle.

Feeling her eyes upon me, I slowly looked up, meeting her gaze.

"That house," I pointed, "this place," I gritted my teeth. "It's suffocating." I stormed away.

———————

I walked over to Max, untied him, and went for a long walk. I needed some time alone. I felt smothered with Cindy around as she could be draining at times. Between her and David, I felt like I had to always be entertaining them. That week made me realize how much I enjoyed being alone and having my thoughts to myself.

When I returned to the house, Cindy was gone. David, too, as his truck wasn't parked in the driveway. I assumed they went off somewhere together. Maybe her fears diminished about the hospital and he took her to see a doctor or perhaps they just went to buy more groceries.

Wherever they went, I'm sure on the way to whatever destination, she was sitting in the passenger seat batting her eyelashes. At that point, I didn't know who or what to believe. Cindy winking at David online on some stupid dating site to test him. Really? Then he called her. I doubt it. I think it was the other way around.

I sensed she had a thing for him right from the start. I remember the way she commented on his looks after finding his business card while poking around in my room. I bet she pursued him and he fell for it, fell for her. She was more his type anyway. They probably set the whole thing up, her surprise visit to see me. I bet he invited her here to replace me.

I walked into the kitchen and looked on the counter to see if she or he or maybe they left me a note. Nope. Nothing. Not even a text on my phone to say, 'be back soon.' The only thing I saw were the sacks of tea tucked in the corner. Conchita's new 'awake' tea.

Grabbing one of the sacks, I untied it and pulled out a teabag. I caught a whiff of lemon and mint as I held it to my nose; it smelled refreshing. Curious about it, I hesitated for a moment, thinking of the side effects of the Tranquilo tea. But it smelled so good and I needed some extra energy, so I figured I'd try some.

While waiting for the water to boil, I gazed out the kitchen window, my eyes falling upon the angel statue. There it stood, smack dab in the middle of the garden between two hibiscus plants—bright pink flowers on one side and pale yellow ones on the other. The kettle soon whistled, jarring me from my thoughts.

After putting a handful of ice cubes in a glass, I poured the tea into it, deciding to make it iced. I took a few sips and it tasted pretty good. It had a certain zing to it. But the tea was still warm; it needed to cool, so I left the glass on the counter and headed back out the door.

When I stepped through the garden, one foot in front of the other, I tried hard not to disturb the freshly seeded plants. As I neared the statue, I noticed something poking up from the ground next to the yellow flowers.

I made my way closer and saw that it was a twig that appeared to have a dot of red paint on it. A marker maybe? Kneeling down, I tugged at the twig and then used it to move some of the soil around. I soon saw the outline of the wooden box but the color was different. It was darker.

Digging with my hands, I pulled it from the ground, rubbing away the dirt covering it. While similar to the other box with its tiny keyhole in the middle, this one was a different box. Carved on top of it was the letter 'S.'

It immediately dawned on me, the name *Susan.*

Suddenly, the air felt thick, heavy. I sat back on my heels, trying to catch my breath as my thoughts whirled in a thousand directions, making me dizzy. Not one wife, but two of them… buried in the garden.

I sat motionless in shock, unable to process the nightmare surrounding me.

David

She's finally gone. I couldn't take another minute or another day. Women like her are all alike; they all have the same agenda. I'll never understand it.

Perhaps I should throw in the towel and be done with them all, and live a quiet, peaceful life in solitude. Well, not entirely, it'll be little ole me alone in the jungle with no one but the birds and other wild creatures. Who needs women anyway? They only complicate things and drive you mad.

An upbeat song starts playing, so I reach down and turn the knob cranking up the volume. With both hands back on the steering wheel, I tap my fingers, keeping tempo with the beat. Salsa music makes me feel alive. I groove in my seat to the sound of the bongos.

Music and a drive, *ahh,* the best therapy there is.

When I arrive back at the house, I catch the sun dipping below the mountains. I gaze at the sky awash with pink and purple hues, breathing in awe at the wondrous sight. It's my favorite time of day, sunset.

I turn off the engine and sit in my truck that I've parked at the bottom of the driveway. From the house, no one can see me here as I'm at another level. The slope of land on my property hides me from view.

Sliding my phone from my pocket, I tap the screen and open the app to see what my Val has been up to today. I glance at the house while waiting for the page to load. It's taking a bit longer than usual.

From the corner of my eye, I see movement. Something has passed by. Craning my neck out the window, I look among the underbrush and see an agouti staring at me. Sitting on its haunches, it munches whatever it's holding in its paws. The cute little critter must've stolen a piece of fruit off the deck.

I love the wildlife here. So many amazing creatures roam the jungle and share my slice of paradise. Too bad Val doesn't feel the same way. I know she's not happy here; her emotions are written all over her face. She doesn't participate in any of my activities; she doesn't seem to enjoy them. She just keeps to herself holed up in the house all day.

The only company of hers is that mutt I found

wandering the streets. Sadly, he's all roly-poly now. She feeds him too much food, always tossing him treats and scraps. Poor boy, I wouldn't want anything to happen to him.

I glance back at my phone. Apparently the camera app does not want to cooperate with me today. Such a shame, I would love to have seen what her day entailed. But at least I know the half of it.

On the drive to the airport, Cindy yapped the entire way. Her mouth was nonstop. She told me all about the hotel and that she needed to get back to work and make more money. Then about all the men who are after her, obviously trying to make me jealous. She went on and on and on. I swear that woman spoke nothing but run-on sentences.

It wasn't until we reached the hairpin turn that I was able to change the subject. After she panicked and dug her nails into my leg while screaming something about driving over the edge.

When I asked about Val, Cindy proceeded to tell me her thoughts. I didn't realize how miserable Val was until Cindy spilled the beans, all the beans. Not a very loyal friend that Cindy, Miss aka CutieC, as she so annoyingly reminded me.

Something tells me that woman is up to no good. I sensed it the first time I met her. I tried my best to be polite, fending off her advances, but she's a bold one that one there. The type who would do anything and everything to get what she wanted, and I mean anything.

I remove the gift bag from the passenger seat and exit

the truck. As I make my way up the walkway, Max starts barking. He can't quite see me yet, but at least he's doing his job.

When I enter the house, I see Val in the kitchen by the sink. She turns, seemingly startled at the sound of the door.

"Hey, where have you been?" she asks, wiping her hands on a dish towel. "Where's Cindy?" She gazes past my shoulder.

"I imagine in the air at the moment."

Tilting her head, she gives me a quizzical look.

"I took her to the airport. She's on her way home," I say, speaking more of Val's language. She's always saying to me… *Can you not be so vague? I need clear and concise communication.* Yes, teacher, I'd like to reply but instead, I just bite my tongue.

"That's weird," she glances around the house as if she doesn't believe me. "She didn't say anything about leaving. As far as I know, she was here for a few more days." Her gaze settles on the bag I'm holding.

Setting the gift bag on the counter, I point to it. "I bought you a little something. I hope you like it."

"Oh, what is it?" She inches near.

"Open it," I order. *How's that for clear and concise*, I'm tempted to say as I watch her cautiously remove the gift from the bag.

Her hands jerk away and she takes a step back, practically leaping in the air. She looks petrified as if I've given her a dead bird or some other deceased animal.

"What's wrong?" I ask. "Don't you like it?"

She lets out a breath and leans over the counter clutching her throat.

I pick up the gift, a small wooden box, my fingers brushing over the hand carving on top. "Look, it even has your initial on it." I smile. "V for Val or if you'd prefer, V for valuables."

I glance at her, and I see that she's shaking like a leaf.

"It's a jewelry box," I say, lifting the lid to reveal the tiny key hiding inside. "You can lock it to keep your things safe," I wink.

I patiently wait for her to say something, anything. Maybe a 'that's nice,' or a 'how thoughtful,' or even a simple 'thank you' would do.

But nope, she doesn't say a word, zip, zilch, nada.

She just stands there, pressing her lips together as though she's never seen anything like it before.

Valerie

I was shaken to the core. I didn't know what to say when David presented me with the jewelry box because it looked exactly like the other two boxes buried in the garden.

Was it some sort of sick joke he was playing? Was he about to do away with me? Turn me into some memory by filling the box with photos of me and locks of my hair.

It was that moment I knew I had to leave while I was still in one piece.

Cindy wasn't returning any of my texts or emails, so I figured she was still upset with me.

I prayed I would hear from her soon as I needed a huge favor. I had to borrow some money since I only had fifty dollars in cash. I had tried ordering another ATM card, but it was conveniently lost in the mail.

David controlled everything. He paid the bills and bought all the groceries. He said he'd take care of me and that I didn't need any money. I guess he thought I'd never want to leave. And in some sense... strangely, I didn't want to.

After six months in Costa Rica, I had nothing to go back to... no job, no roommate, and no house. But staying with him had become too risky with unease and unknowns lurking around every corner. Too many things just weren't adding up.

If David was starting a tea business with Conchita, why did he need me? Did he want me to be some test dummy for his tea recipes? To see if I'd survive the next new and improved brew? Why was everything so secretive?

I couldn't help think there was more to it, that something terrible might have happened at the house. *I need to get to the bottom of this*, I had said to myself.

"Need to get to the bottom of what?" David asked, his voice coming from behind me.

I couldn't believe he had heard me. I must've spoken the words out loud. At that point, I had nothing else to lose. I only wanted the truth. I wanted him to come clean about everything.

"David..." I began, unsure of what to say or ask.

"Val, are you unhappy here?"

"I want to be happy. I just don't understand what's

going on."

"What do you mean?"

"I have a confession," I said, wringing my hands. "I was in the garden… and I found—"

"I know," he interrupted.

I was startled by the way he looked at me.

"I saw the footprints, both sets—the paw prints and imprints from your boots. I know you and Max were in the garden."

"Yeah, he was off the leash and dug something up."

"The box?"

"One of them but I know there are two."

"I was going to tell you eventually. Show you where I keep my stash."

"Stash?"

"Yes, Val, my money," he said reluctantly.

"Oh."

"Why the face?"

"I figured… I thought you were keeping something else in those boxes."

"Like what?"

"Oh, I don't know… dead bodies maybe."

"Dead bodies!" His jaw dropped as he threw his head back. "Val, you can't be serious?"

My silence told him I was.

"First of all, please tell me how a body would even fit into a box that size?"

"I figured maybe you burnt them."

"Burnt them?" he gasped. "I hope you mean burnt as in cremated."

"My gosh, David, you put an angel in the middle of the garden. The boxes, the flowers, the statue... it looks like a mini-cemetery out there. What else was I supposed to think?"

"You should've asked instead of thinking and then you would've known."

"But the boxes, one has an 'S' and the other a 'G.' Those letters are the initials of your wives... your ex-wives, right?"

"Yes, but they also stand for silver and gold." He glared at me. "I worry about that mind of yours... always conjuring up things that aren't real."

"Then what about the insurance papers in the cardboard box with my name on them."

"What insurance papers with your name?"

"I saw a folder with my name written on it. Inside were papers, some kind of insurance policy... granted they were written in Spanish, but I know what I saw." Crossing my arms, I waited for his answer.

"That's the policy on this house," he yelled, pointing to the floor, then at me, "not you!" He ran a hand through his hair. "Maybe I scribbled your name on it because I was thinking about you that day when I was on the phone with the insurance company."

I stood there watching him furiously pace the room. I felt silly, ashamed of myself. I didn't know how I had gotten things so wrong. But there was still another piece of the puzzle to be solved.

"Seriously, Val, you need to lay off the mystery movies. Clearly, you've been watching too many."

I took a deep breath, gathering my thoughts. "Then what about the letter I found in the box?"

"The letter?" he spun around. "Now there's a letter? Let me guess, with your name on it or some other secret code."

"Actually, yes, it's addressed to D from G. So I imagine it's to you from your ex."

He walked over to the sliding glass door, placing his fingers on the handle.

"So you found the letter." Opening the door, he looked over his shoulder. "You're quite the sleuth, aren't you?"

"Did something happen here at the house?"

He looked away and then walked out onto the deck. I followed him.

"The other day," I said, catching up to him. "The look on your face when Cindy almost fell. I can't help but feel that something happened here."

He sat down next to some banana peels near the end of the deck. With his legs dangling, he picked up one of the peels, hurling it in the air. My heart skipped a beat as I watched his body lean over a bit too far. I rushed over to him, grabbing him in fear he would fall.

"It should have been me that day," he said, placing his hand on my arm. "It was an accident, a horrible accident." Chewing his lower lip, his eyes welled with tears.

"I'm so sorry." I let out a breath, crouching down next to him. We sat there for a few moments staring off in the distance and up at the canopy of trees.

"Maybe it was a bad idea for me to come here," I said.

He sat quietly, swinging his legs, and then picked at another banana peel.

"I think I should leave and give you some space." I started to stand up.

"But you have nowhere else to go," he sniffled.

"I guess I can go back to Vegas and stay with Cindy. After all, I did share a house with her."

"But this is your home now... our home," he looked at me. "This house is all we have."

I wanted to tell him it didn't feel like our home. It never did. It always felt like someone else was there watching us —as if a presence was hovering over us.

"If you want me to stay, I need to know what happened... about the accident."

Inhaling and exhaling, his chest heaved slowly as he closed his eyes.

"My ex and I... we had an argument one night..."

"So you lived here before... with her... in this house." The puzzle had just become more complicated.

"She was drinking tea and taunting me."

The tea, *not new,* I added to my mental notes while waiting for him to continue. I watched as he put his hand to his forehead running it down his face.

He let out a tense breath. "And then she..."

David

I need something to calm my nerves. If I reveal the story, the whole story, no doubt she will leave. I thought we had a chance... that I had the chance to build something new.

I glance over at Val and she shoots me a nervous stare.

I thought I had finally found the right woman, a woman who could stand the test of time. My heart fills with dread and my head starts to pound as I search for the right words to explain what happened. No matter what I say or how I say it, Val will come to her own conclusion.

Did you know that when two people hear the same thing, they hear it differently? It happens because we process things through our own perceptions, our own filters.

I know for a fact because I had two wives who were completely oblivious to what I would say. In the end, they only heard what they wanted to hear but it wasn't the truth… my truth.

"Maybe we should have some wine," I say.

"Now?" Val makes a face. I watch as she walks over to the bamboo dining set, taking a seat in the yellow chair, always the same yellow chair.

I stand up and walk through the open glass door and into the kitchen. At least ten bugs are buzzing around my head because Val not only forgot to close the glass door but also left the screen door open. She's always complaining about not enough air circulation and has all the ceiling fans set on high. She completely forgets that it only takes a minute for the house to be swarming with insects. She's slipping. Or maybe she wants me to be eaten alive.

I swat at my arm, scratching intensely as a red bump appears. These bugs seem to love me more than Val or maybe they just don't like her overwhelming vanilla body lotion. Everything around here reeks of vanilla: vanilla candles, soaps, sprays, and perfumes.

I think back to that night at dinner with the gals in LA. *"You're no fun. You're so vanilla,"* Cindy had mocked, calling her 'vanilla Val.' Maybe she's right. I laugh to myself. 'Vanilla Val' does sort of fit her personality.

I gaze at the wine rack and sigh. We're out of red. Only one bottle lies there and it's white. Do I dare? Tapping a finger on my lip, I ponder a moment.

Yanking the bottle off the rack, I grip its neck and turn the cap. The cap twists too easily as if it hadn't been properly sealed. I pause for a second, slightly suspicious, but then one of them must have opened it the other night and decided not to drink it. We had all been over our limit and had imbibed too much.

"I think I should give you some space." Val's words ring in my head. So lame, so original. I scoff at her feeble attempt to leave me. If she thinks she can just scurry back to Vegas, back to Cindy and her old life, she's crazy. It's funny how Cindy made a little joke saying that I should be in her life. She said I had chosen the wrong woman and I should have picked her.

I knew she had a thing for me, but didn't realize it was so serious. She practically undressed me on the ride to the airport and made it crystal clear she doesn't want Val to return to Vegas. She was 'over her,' she said, with a definitive tone in her voice. Either Val is lying to me about going back to live with Cindy or the poor girl has no clue.

Reaching for two glasses, I grab the bottle and head back out to the deck. Now I have two stories to share with Val, but I'm not sure how I'll break the news. She's sitting there picking at her cuticles, a bad habit she can't seem to break.

"So," I say, pouring the wine, filling our glasses. I place one in front of Val and she slides it to the side.

"Are you not going to join me?" Taking a sip, I wince. It's a tad bitter. I pull out a green chair settling into it.

"I've had enough wine for a while," she turns away.

"But it's white, your favorite." I hold up my glass, willing her to pick up hers so we can clink and say cheers like the good old times. "Speaking of favorites, if you don't mind me asking, why do you always sit in the yellow chair?"

Her gaze is solemn and a veil of sadness covers her face. She looks as if she's given up on us. I sit quietly studying her, sipping my wine despite the taste.

"Why did you search for deadly concoctions?" she says out of nowhere.

For a split second, I am stunned. How could she know that?

"Are you... are you trying to poison someone?" she fearfully stutters. "Are you trying to poison me?"

"No! Val! What are you thinking?"

"I'm repeating what I saw on my computer... your search history," she flinches.

"What you saw was me checking to make sure I had the right mixture... a safe mixture. I was not concocting anything deadly."

"What mixture?"

"The tea, Val, the tea. What else would I be mixing?" My blood pressure rises and I feel it rushing through my veins. I reach for the bottle almost knocking it over and pour myself another glass of wine. My hands tremble. "Why do you keep looking at me like that?"

"Like what?" she says, narrowing her eyes. "Like a

woman who doesn't know what the heck is going on around here. Like a woman who doesn't know who or what to believe… yeah, that would be me." She shifts in her seat, and everything is blurry. "So let me get this straight," she huffs. "You already knew Conchita, before we arrived here?"

"Yes."

"And your ex knew Conchita too."

"Yes," a stab of pain slashes the side of my head.

"And this tea business is not new. You and Conchita have been brewing things up for a while now."

I nod while massaging the sides of my temples.

"And you had a fight with your ex who was drinking the tea."

"She went crazy! She went crazy from drinking the tea." Leaping from my seat, the chair tips over as I stumble.

"I told you she was prodding me. She was jealous. She was jealous of everything, of me, of my tea, of my relationship with Conchita. She wanted to be the one who created the tea."

I watch Val lift the chair off the ground and put it back in its place. Why is she doing it in slow motion?

"She started mixing her own blends, her own mishmash of herbs and flowers. I didn't know about it and she didn't know what she was doing." I stop for a moment to catch my breath. "She wanted to prove she could do it better, better than everyone else." My head is pounding so loudly I guzzle the rest of my wine.

"Easy on the wine, David," I hear her say. "I think you've had enough."

"You know, for once you're right. I don't feel so good. I need to lie down." I stagger into the living room and fall onto the futon. I watch as the ceiling fan goes round and round, making me dizzy. My body feels weak and everything is hazy.

"I didn't kill her," I whisper.

"What? What did you say?" Val's voice is muffled and she sounds far away.

"She pushed me. She was always pushing my buttons. But that day, she pushed me to the edge, so I pushed back." I feel myself fading.

"Maybe I pushed," I muster a breath, "a little too far..."

39

Valerie

He pushed her during an argument. He said he didn't kill her but she's dead.

I stood there frozen, my stomach roiling in fear as I stared at David out cold on the futon. I watched as his chest rose slightly, up and then down, making sure he was breathing… making sure he was still alive.

After hearing his confession before he passed out, it was time to get out of there. But my body felt heavy, weighed down with so much grief for both of us. I had to leave the man I loved, a man whose ex-wife, accident or not, was dead.

I went into the bedroom, swung open the closet doors,

and grabbed a suitcase. As I stood there throwing my clothes on the bed, my heart ached but the voice inside my head screamed. *Get out now!* After stuffing my clothes in the suitcase, I gathered my items from the bathroom counter, tossing them in my bag.

I needed to get out of the house quickly before David woke up. If I stayed, I wouldn't have known what to say or do. Even worse, I may never have had the chance to leave. Reaching for my phone, I called a taxi and then went to the kitchen to pack Max's things. He was my dog, after all, and I had promised I'd always take care of him. He'd have a much better life with me not tied to a dog run for umpteen hours a day.

I softly padded over to David one last time to check on him. Snoring away, he had changed positions and I figured he'd be waking up soon. I left him a note on the counter to say goodbye.

With my bags in hand, I went outside, propping them by the door while I rushed over to the dog house David had built. Max heard me and came out of his house, wagging his tail, excited to see me. I was so happy to see him and even happier when I untied him from the run for the last time.

Max was soon by my side trotting along as I strolled down the driveway, the wheels on my suitcase bouncing along the gravel. Although I was leaving the house, I hadn't planned on leaving Costa Rica. There was no way I was going back to Vegas, that was for sure. I remembered seeing a help wanted sign posted the last time I was in town. A new hotel was opening up by the beach and they were hiring servers and bartenders. The sign had read, *debe hablar inglés*, must speak English. I figured Max and I could find a little place and run around barefoot in the sand. Live that simple, carefree life I had once dreamed about long ago.

Halfway to the road, I spotted a colorful butterfly sitting on a leaf. I stopped to look at it but it didn't even move. It was as if it was watching me or wanted to be noticed.

Its vibrant colors made me think of the flowers David had sent to me at the hotel. Red-tipped yellow roses—for happiness, friendship, and new beginnings. Tears pricked my eyes and I momentarily thought of turning around. I thought back to the room I stayed in at Villa Manuela on my first trip with David to Costa Rica. The lovely room with the bright yellow décor. I have so many memories of our vacation.

Then I remembered the little yellow bird I had found at the house that day, talking to it and feeding it some fruit on the deck. I loved watching the birds and listening to them sing. Rain or shine, there was always a creature to see through the many glass doors of the house.

It was funny when David asked me, 'Why do you always sit in the yellow chair?' The color, I wanted to say, reminded me of the joyful times in our relationship. Yellow is the color of contentment, optimism, and sunshine, all things I had wished for and wanted in my life. That day, however, as I walked away, yellow only stood for remembrance.

I glanced back at the butterfly now fluttering its wings. Within seconds it took flight, hovering in front of me, and then flying away. I took it as a sign. It was time for me, too, to fly away.

When we reached the end of the driveway, the taxi was parked there waiting for me. The driver loaded my luggage into the trunk while Max and I hopped in the back seat.

Did I really know who David was? Truly understand the person underneath the handsome exterior? At times he seemed like a tortured soul and other times, a savior. Like a knight in shining armor, he had entered the hotel that day and swept me off my feet. He whisked me away, far away, into his world, to his 'little slice of paradise' as he always referred to it.

I gazed over my shoulder and watched as the glass house faded away further into the jungle. As I turned back and looked at the road ahead of me, a quote I once saw came to mind. Forcing a half smile, I recited the words in my head.

'Sometimes, you just have to write your own damn fairy tale.'

40

David

'Look, I'm an angel,' she says. Twirling around with her arms open wide, she waves them in the air gently by her side. 'See my wings, watch me fly.'

'Be careful,' I say, 'you're standing too close to the edge.'

'Why, oh why, does time pass me by? Why does my love not want me to fly?' Whispering the words in a heavenly voice, there's a distant look in her eye. She's the saddest, most beautiful angel I've ever seen.

I watch as she whirls and floats through the air as a trumpet sounds in the distance. One last twirl, her figure unravels as she slowly fades away.

I open my eyes and blink at the ceiling. My limbs feel numb. I'm hot and sticky, drenched in sweat. My head pounds loudly thumping in my ears. I must have been dreaming, but it felt so real.

She was here with me, back at the house, the house I built for her.

I had given her everything I had but it still wasn't enough. From the moment I laid eyes on her, I knew she was the one. So innocent and so pure, I had to protect her while I could.

I think back to that night when I first met Slim. He introduced me to someone he thought could help, a kind, little Indian lady with an herb garden and a knack for brewing tea. He said her blends might help cure my ailing wife.

For a while, I thought they would help calm her, help ease her pain. But unknown to me, behind my back, she started mixing her own blends. She thought she'd do it her way by formulating her own tea to make herself better.

At first, I didn't know what flowers and herbs she was using. But then that day, that ill-fated day, I still can't shake it from my mind. The day I found out she had been mixing angel trumpets in her tea.

"Angel trumpets?" I asked, alarmed when she first told me.

"Yes, darling, the beautiful bell-shaped flowers that grow along the pathway. The pretty one's that hang upside down." With a tiny spark in her eye, she smiled.

In full panic, I looked at her in horror. "They're deadly."

Her eyes fluttered in a cloud of confusion. "How could something so lovely be so lethal?"

I remember that she had become paranoid and was hallucinating. She kept seeing things that weren't there. At first, I thought it was caused by her illness, but tragically, she was slowly poisoning herself.

My beautiful, sweet, Susan ripped from my life too soon. We were meant to be together forever.

There's a sound coming from outside, from out on the deck—a scratching-like scraping of a chair. From where I lay, I can see the curtains are drawn. One of the glass doors is slightly ajar, the bottom of the curtain blowing in the breeze.

I glance up at the clock on the wall. Val must be outside enjoying the last rays of the sun before it sets. For a moment, I wonder why I'm here in the living room and not in bed.

The last thing I remember is drinking wine with Val out on the deck. Maybe I passed out from a few too many. It wouldn't be the first time. My head is still hurting as I make a mental note never to drink white wine again.

My mouth is dry and a bitter taste coats my tongue. What I need right now is some water, a glass of cold water. Then I'll be ready to clear the air and be honest with Val.

As I move my arms to hoist myself up, I can't. There's a clanging of metal, something cold, hard tugging on my wrists. Blinking my eyes, I see handcuffs and chains. I'm shackled to the arms of the futon.

Is Val playing a prank? Is this a little game gone wrong? But then I tell myself no, it's not something she'd do.

"Val," I call out, hoping she'll hear me. As I twist and turn, I become more frustrated by the second. I can't believe I'm chained to a piece of furniture.

"Hey, Val! Are you out there? This isn't funny. Can you please come in here and help me?"

The curtains move and she appears. I'm shocked beyond belief. She strolls into the room, my heart racing as she stares me down. I can't believe my eyes. Shaking my head, a sudden coldness hits my core.

She can't be here, maybe I'm still dreaming. It's been so long since I've seen her.

"Hello, David," she says, her voice filled with scorn. "Happy to see me?"

"What are you doing here?" I say, flinching, the chains jangling.

"I came here to check on you."

"Stop with the lies! You wanted nothing to do with me. That's why you left."

"You're right. I never was a good liar," she sighs.

"What do you want? What do you want from me?"

"Oh please, spare me the drama. You know damn well what I want." She moves toward me with a scowl. "I want my house back."

"Your house?" I seethe. "It's not your house. It's mine."

"You promised when you dragged me here, it would be ours... our house. But it never was our house, was it, David? It was always hers... your sweet, little wife whose death you never got over."

"Get out!"

"She's the woman you really built this house for, isn't she?"

"I said, get out!"

"You can't make me. You have nothing. You have nothing left."

"Oh, shut up, you stupid bitch."

"What are you going to do now, David? Hmm? Now that your little Val is gone." She smirks.

"Gone? What do you mean she's gone? How do you know about Val? How do you know her name?"

"I know everything. You're not the only one who has hidden cameras around here."

"Did you hurt her? Did you do something to Val?"

"Relax, David. She left on her own. And you'll be happy to know she took the dog with her." Cocking her head, she mimics me, "Oh Max, is that you?"

"It was you that night when I called for Max after he ran off. You were here, outside the house, snooping around, spying on me."

She stares at me with a sardonic grin. The strap of her purse slides from her shoulder and she quickly adjusts it, holding it tight to her side.

"You never left, did you? You've been here all along in

Costa Rica this whole time." I snarl, waiting for a reply. "Answer me!"

"Calm down, David, perhaps you need something to settle your nerves. How about I make you a cup of tea?"

"Just leave, will you."

"Or have you still not perfected the blend yet. After all this time, I thought you would have found the right one by now… the right tea… the right woman."

"Stop goading me, or else."

"Or else what, David? Are you threatening me?"

I take a deep breath. "Just free me from these damn chains."

She stands there, leering while reaching for something in her purse. The keys, I hope, for the handcuffs. As soon as she releases me I'm going to wipe that evil grin from her face forever.

There's a knock on the front door and her head whips in that direction.

"Oh gawd, please don't tell me she's back," she says.

"Untie me, unlock me so I can answer the door," I demand.

"You're not going anywhere." She pulls out a gun aiming it straight at my face. "One word and you and that girlfriend of yours are dead."

I stare down the barrel and swallow in fear. I can't believe what is happening—a nightmare come true.

"I'm serious, David, I'm done with your games. One

word, one peep from you when I open that door and Val will be gone forever."

I stare into her dark, flat eyes; there's nothing behind them. She's clearly gone insane.

"Do you hear me?" She waves the gun at me. "Do you understand?"

I nod. I obey her command only because of Val, my love, my light. I would kill myself if something ever happened to her.

She heads toward the door and I crane my neck hoping to get a glimpse of Val. But the damn kitchen island blocks my view; I want to kick myself for building it so big. I listen as the door opens and closes. I want to scream, but I bite my tongue in silence and wait.

I think of Val, her beautiful smile, and all the memorable times we shared, the scenes flashing through my mind like a movie. I can still remember the look on her face when I brought her here. When she first saw the house and gazed upon the windows, I recall the words as if she'd said them yesterday.

"What's with all the bars?" she asked. "It looks like a jail cell."

Today, sadly, I'd have to agree.

41

Cindy

I stand outside your house knocking on your door. I'm so nervous right now and hope I'm not making a mistake. I try thinking of what I'll say when you open the door but my stomach is tied in knots and words escape me. I'm not exactly sure how you'll react.

I can't help wonder if Val's okay but I also can't lie. I hope she's gone by now. Long gone. After spiking her white wine with your tea and my sleeping pills, I'm sure her little nightmares have sent her running away, far away… it's what she does best.

See, I know my Val, better than you do, David. I tried telling you that when I was here last time. Val has trust issues. She cracks under pressure and doesn't like being controlled. Sure she comes across all nice and sweet, but if you disappoint that woman or break her trust, believe me, you will have hell to pay.

I never thought you two were meant for each other. You were not a good match, no siree. I am more your type and you know it. For some reason, though, you can't seem to admit it. I wonder why.

Do I remind you of someone? One of your ex-wives maybe? I heard all about them. Val told me everything. She thinks something happened here to one of them or both. But I'm not so sure. Maybe you're just heartbroken and need more time to heal. You'll be okay. I can help soothe your pain. We all carry emotional baggage and I'm ready and willing to help you with yours.

So here I am, standing on your doorstep, ready to share my life with you. Because the moment I saw you and saw this house... I fell in love with you both.

Raising my hand, it trembles as I knock on the door again. I hope you're home. I'm so excited to see your face.

EPILOGUE

When I opened the door, I saw some blonde chick standing there. I told her David had left the premises and that he didn't live here anymore. I then informed her that the house was mine and that it was never his to begin with.

At first she didn't believe me. We argued for a while and then she broke down in tears and refused to leave. But when I said I'd call the police and report her for trespassing, she ran off. I'm pretty sure I won't be seeing any more of her.

When I first told Slim I wanted to leave, he said I should wait and think it through. I didn't know if he could keep a secret, but he promised to keep me safe until I was sure of my decision, so he offered me a place to stay in one of the casitas at his lodge.

As time passed, I had regrets about leaving and I started plotting my return. But when David suddenly came back unannounced, he threw a wrench in my plans.

Yes, I was there the night they arrived. I saw them get out of the truck. When Slim took a closer look at her, he told me she looked a lot like me. I couldn't believe it, so I had to see it for myself. That's when I began stalking them.

I was angry at first because he had replaced me so easily. Even more so because his replacement looked like me. But as I watched them come and go, Val appeared to be less and less happy as the days passed. I figured David was keeping the same secrets from her as he had from me.

Such as the interesting fact that he built this house in the exact same place as the first one. The tiny blue house where he lost his wife, Susan. She wasn't well, the poor dear. I heard how she struggled with dreadful delusions. David said she would continuously rant about being haunted by previous tenants. He said she could never quite see out of that house despite the beautiful view, so he promised to build her a new one, a house with great big windows. But sadly, he was too late.

One night, she had a horrible accident. I heard she was drinking tea and dancing on the deck. The poor thing unfortunately drank the wrong brew and twirled herself right off the deck. At least, that's what David told me... his version of the story.

Soon after the tragedy, David went into a deep depression. He blamed himself for her death. He regretted introducing her to Slim, Conchita, and the tea. He was never able to forgive himself for not building the new house in time.

When I first met David, I had tried helping him with his sorrows. I helped him design this house, our new home, to honor her memory. Soon after, however, his sadness turned to control. I think it was the way he coped. He then became determined to help Conchita with her struggling tea business as she too was burdened with guilt. He said if they mixed the ingredients correctly, they could help many people with their assorted ailments.

Slim mentioned they were working on some new kind of tea called 'awake.' Supposedly it could help you see into the future. Imagine that. I mean, I've heard about reading tea leaves before, but drinking tea to see what the future holds? Who would have thought it was possible?

But I'm rambling now, so back to the house—my house. You see, David never got over losing sweet Susan. Sadly, she was the source of our contention and one day I snapped. I simply couldn't take it anymore. I had finally had enough.

Although David pushed me away, I loved this house. It was the only thing that made me happy. So I hatched a plan to take it back. But thanks to Val, I didn't need to execute it. She made it really easy for me, and I can never thank her enough.

I watched as she tried solving the puzzle, becoming frustrated and finally giving up. The day she departed was the day I returned. She left the door open, actually unlocked, and I walked right into the house. I was surprised to find David passed out and thankful I didn't have to use the gun.

So here I am, back at my house.

By now you've probably figured out who I am. Yes, it's me, Gina, wife number two. While I may be his second, I will be his last.

David may not have been happy to see me, and quite frankly, I'm not sure if I'm happy to see him. Perhaps we'll find a way to make it work. Maybe I'll give him a second chance... I'm still thinking about it. At any rate, it's so good to be back at my house—the beautiful glass house of my dreams.

Where you can see in and I can see out—forever.

A NOTE FROM BETTINA

Thank you so much for taking the time to read The Glass House.

I would like to know your thoughts about the book and would love to hear from you. To connect and stay in touch, please visit me at bettinawolfe.com.

If you enjoyed this book and have a few moments to spare, I would appreciate it if you could leave a review. Reviews are not only helpful for me, but they also help others who may be interested in reading this book.

Please note a portion of the proceeds go toward local animal rescues.

Once again, thank you for reading The Glass House.

Until the next story,

Bettina

ACKNOWLEDGMENTS

A heartfelt thank you to the following people for helping me bring this book to life. I am beyond grateful for all of you.

To Judy Worman, thank you for editing my manuscript, and for your expertise and guidance throughout the entire process.

To Stuart Bache and the team at Books Covered, thank you for an amazing cover.

A special thanks to my best friend and partner in crime. I appreciate your encouragement, patience, and unwavering support. I couldn't do it without you.

ABOUT THE AUTHOR

Bettina Wolfe has been creating characters and dreaming up stories for as long as she can remember. When she's not writing, she's reading and loves a good mystery. Originally from the East Coast, she now lives in the Southwest.

Made in the USA
Middletown, DE
17 December 2020